# Sweet Surrender

## NAIMA SIMONE

# DEDICATION

To Gary. 143.

# ACKNOWLEDGMENTS

First, thank you to my Father, and that I can always look to the hills—to You—for my help.

Gary, thank you for having faith bigger than a mustard seed. You are my inspiration in my books and in life. And you make the perfect cup of coffee! Eden Royce. Thank you for your editing expertise! I loved working with you!

Debra Glass. This cover! Sigh. And just…everything. You've been so selfless with your knowledge, your talent and yourself. A bestie and guru all rolled into one. And beware. I'm in your life for always. Just thought I'd warn you ahead of time…

Jessica Lee and Dahlia Rose. Ladies, if not for you and our writing challenges, I might still be playing a rousing game of Pet Rescue. LOL! Thank you for pushing and, well, challenging me. Let's keep it up!

Stormy Pate. Thank you for always being so willing to beta read! When I receive your thumb's up, I know the book is ready for the world. You're simply awesome!

Thank you to the Saints and Sinners for always being a bright spot in every day! The laughter and support I receive from you guys keep me pumped and sitting in that writing chair. Finding that special group of ladies who share your kind of crazy is invaluable! LOL! Love y'all!

# SWEET SURRENDER

Killing the messenger is frowned upon. Okay, then... What about laying the messenger on the nearest flat surface and making her scream with pleasure?

From the moment Hayden Reynolds approaches Griffin Sutherland in the local, Florida dive bar, all he can think about is fisting her dark curls and stroking those gorgeous curves. But hell would freeze over before she allowed him to touch her because she's the woman he left behind five years earlier. And now she's there to deliver a message— an ultimatum—from his estranged father. Blackmail forces Griffin, black sheep of his powerful Texas family, back home to play nice. But the terms of his bargain say nothing about not satisfying his need for the woman he's never forgotten...never stopped wanting...

Hayden is no longer the naive girl who once fiercely loved a golden Sutherland and believed he and a maid's daughter could live happily ever after. Griffin broke her all those years ago, but she forced herself to pick up the pieces and move on. Now he's back in Texas, acting the part of the proper, dutiful son. But there's nothing proper about the detailed—dirty—descriptions of how he wants to touch her...take her... Though her body heats every time he's near, she refuses to surrender to his special brand of passion. Griffin may have returned home, but he's leaving again. And this time he won't take her heart with him...

# CHAPTER ONE

"I'm leaving."

The low murmur assaulted Hayden Reynolds' ears as if it'd been shouted with a megaphone. Her heart, which had just begun to slow from the after effects of a blistering orgasm, sped up again, pounding against her sternum like a caged wild thing. A sickening tension invaded her body, chasing away the delicious, warm lethargy that always followed making love with Griffin Sutherland. From the first time eight months ago, to the last time three minutes ago, he'd never failed to make her body sing. But now, two words had struck a discordant chord, and it reverberated through her like a sharp, painful note.

"Hayden?"

Rolling over, she clutched the sheet to her chest, wrapping it around her hips. She sat, one hand gripping the cover to her breasts, and the other curled over the edge of the mattress as if it were the only thing keeping her anchored. Keeping her from falling over into the dark hole of pain and loneliness that had suddenly yawned open at her feet.

"I heard you," she said, amazed at her calm tone. "When?"

"Tomorrow."

*God. Tomorrow?* She stifled a gasp. She could count down the time she had left with him in hours and minutes. That explained why he'd shown up at the door of her small apartment without calling. Why there'd been a sense of urgency in his lovemaking. No. Not lovemaking. Sex. A person didn't make love to someone they planned on leaving...on abandoning.

"So what was this, then? A good-bye fuck?" This time she couldn't prevent the hurt from thickening her voice. Grief started clawing at her throat, determined to leave her in an anguished rush. Swallowing convulsively, she shoved it back down.

"No. Yes. *Shit.*"

The mattress dipped as he erupted from the bed. And damn her, she couldn't help but glance over her shoulder and stare as he picked up his earlier discarded jeans and dragged them up his legs and hips. Even with pain burrowing deeper and deeper into her heart, arousal snaked through her, heating her blood, tightening her belly.

Moonlight streamed through the windows of her bedroom, gilding him in its pearlescent beam. Emphasizing the masculine beauty of his strong, broad shoulders, wide chest and ridged abdomen. Unable to help herself, she lowered her gaze to the flat belly and narrow hips where the defined vee only the truly cut sported arrowed into his unbuttoned jeans. At that moment, the Greek mythology stories she loved to read flooded her mind. The tales of the untouchable, powerful, beautiful gods who ruled from on high and sometimes blessed humans with their favor. That's what Griffin was. A god.

A Sutherland.

And she was the poor, foolish human girl who dared to believe she could capture the heart of one.

Screw foolish. Somewhere in a village there was a Missing Idiot poster with her picture on it tacked to a lamp post.

She snatched the sheet off, and for a moment she fought the tangled material strangling her legs. *Calm down*, a voice warned. But she didn't heed it as she finally tore free and grabbed her robe off the floor.

"Baby, please, listen to me," Griff whispered, rounding the end of the queen-sized bed that took up most of the space in the small room.

"Why didn't you tell me?" She shrugged into the robe and tugged the sash tight, tying it in jerky movements. Then she gripped the lapels close at her throat, an arm circling her waist, shielding herself from the one person she'd never thought she would have to protect herself from.

"Because I just decided it today. But, Hayden, you more than anyone know how much I hate it here. I've been slowly suffocating with my father, the business…" He shoved his fingers through his thick, golden waves, fisting the strands tight at the base of his skull. "I'm twenty-five, and I don't know what it's like to be my own man. To be something other than my family name. To have a job I love and earned instead of inherited. I need to leave or else become someone I don't know. Or worse. Hate."

Yes, she knew everything he'd stated. She was a student at Rice University working her way toward a Bachelor's in Managerial Studies, but she already possessed a Ph.D. in Griffin Sutherland. Had been an avid student from the second she'd met the devilish eleven-year-old son of the wealthy family her mother had been hired to work for as a housekeeper. At eleven, Griff had been a hellion, and while he'd matured through the years, he'd never lost that sense of rebellion. While his older brother Joshua and younger sister Callie had toed the Sutherland line of decorum, proper deportment and obedience, Griff had seemed to glory in touting it. He'd scratched at the Sutherland skin, itching to find his own way, his own path that didn't include the well-travelled one his father Joshua Sutherland, Sr., youngest son of Texas oil baron Bud Sutherland, had set out for him. At twenty-five, he chafed at the demands placed on him, and in the last six months, that restlessness and dissatisfaction had intensified. Objectively, his announcement shouldn't surprise her. But, oh God, it did. It wrecked her.

Because she'd allowed herself to fall in love with him. Fall so deeply, the thought of waking up tomorrow and acknowledging he was gone tore at her with greedy, vicious claws.

"Have you told your father yet?"

Griff nodded, his mouth firming into a straight line while his eyes blazed blue fire. "Yes, before I came here. He told me if I leave not to come back."

In spite of her own pain, her heart ached for him. "Griff, I'm sorry…"

He shook his head, slicing a hand through the air. "Forget it. He reacted exactly how I expected. I don't need his money or connections anyway. They come with strings, and I'm trying to escape his control and influence." A hard smile curved his sensual mouth. "Besides, he still has the heir, he doesn't need the spare. You're the only one I had left to tell."

"Where are you going?" she rasped.

"Florida, I think. We have distant cousins there. It's a starting place, at least."

Florida. Damn near across the country. So far. So far from her...

"Take me with you." The words exploded past her lips before she could trap them. But once they were out, she couldn't rescind them. No. No. She meant them. "I-I can go with you." She hurried across the few feet separating them and clutched his arm, the heat from his body searing her palm. "Please, Griff. We can leave toge—"

"No, Hayden."

Just that firm denial. Not even unkind, but gentle. Hell, a part of her wished the rejection had been harsh, mean. Because the soft tone smacked too close to pity. And like salt rubbed into an open wound, it was agony to her pride, her heart.

"You have one more year left of school." He cupped her jaw, smoothed his thumb over her chin.

She shook her head. "I don't care. I can finish online—"

"And what about the Meyers internship? That's an honor and a once in a lifetime opportunity, and you worked damn hard to win it."

Only two business students out of the thousands who applied for the prestigious internship program won it. Hayden had been chosen—one of the first women to be selected in the past five years, and the first Latina in the history of the program. During her senior year, she would work in a Fortune 500 company headquartered in Houston, earning invaluable experience and connections in the field she hoped to be employed in one day. When she'd been notified of her acceptance two weeks ago, she'd been ecstatic. Now, staring at the resolve in Griffin's eyes, she resented it.

"I can't let you throw away all your hard work to follow me," Griffin murmured. "You've worked too hard, put in too much time."

"I don't—"

"No, baby."

Still in that awful, terrible, tender voice. And under it, she caught not just the resolution, but the determination.

The finality.

Jerking free of his hold, she stumbled backward before catching herself. Murmuring her name, he reached out to steady her, but she flinched from his touch.

"You have no idea how much I want to—"

"Stop it," she ordered, slamming up her hand, palm out. "You've never lied to me, so please don't start now." Inhaling, she welcomed—finally—the numbness that eased in, coating the gnawing, pulsing pain and grief in a cool wash of white. Sealing it until later when he wasn't standing in front of her, and she could crash into pieces without him as a witness. "I shouldn't have asked you to take me with you. It was unfair," she apologized, the flat tone a far cry from the desperate one of moments ago. "You're right. I've always known how unhappy you were here, and you never made any promises to me."

Silence permeated the room. The occasional honk of a passing car as well as snatches of conversation and laughter probably from students returning home after hitting the bars filtered up to her bedroom, punctuating the thick quiet.

"Look at me, Hayden," he quietly demanded. Helpless to resist, she shifted her gaze from the base of his throat to his face. His hooded stare and tense, too-still frame reminded her of a predator about to leap on its prey. "Care to explain that?"

An unbidden shiver tripped over her skin at the dark, faintly ominous question that wasn't a question but an order. Disgust curdled in her belly. Because even as he stood here cracking her heart in two, he excited her, sent desire skating through her.

God, she was pathetic.

Crossing the room toward her dresser, she shrugged a shoulder. "Just what I said. You made no promises. And we both knew there was an expiration date on…this." She jerked open a drawer and withdrew a t-shirt and shorts. It was one o'clock in the morning, but she needed more cover than the flimsy robe. More armor. Besides, she wouldn't be getting any more sleep tonight.

"This?" he repeated, his voice closer.

She stiffened, momentarily pausing before stepping into the shorts and pulling them on. Only then did she remove the robe and let it slide down her arms, keeping her back to him.

"Yes, this. Friends with benefits. Fuck buddies. Whatever you want to call it." The lies tasted like the filthiest of ashes on her tongue. The past eight months hadn't been just a casual passing of time filled with friendly fucking. For her, it'd been…*everything.*

He'd catapulted her to a world where she'd transformed into a carnal creature that craved every erotic, dirty thing he said and did to her body with a need veering close to addiction. Instilled in her a feminine confidence that changed her, emboldened her. Wrapped her in a security that she'd felt free to explore and indulge her every fantasy without fear of judgment or recrimination.

He'd made her feel wanted, beautiful...loved.

But apparently, it'd all been a figment of her infatuated virgin's imagination.

"You're going to want to shut up now." The low growl had her stomach tightening, her sex pulsing. Her nipples beaded against the cotton of the shirt she'd tugged down. She sank her teeth into her bottom lip, trapping the moan begging to escape. Only he had this effect on her. Could make her ache with just his voice. It was his super power and her kryptonite.

"Why?" she pressed, bitterness escaping the numbness in her chest and creeping into her voice. Part of her needed to poke him, shove him. Needed to hear him admit she'd been a fling, a fuck toy. Needed him to hurt her so badly with his words that this messy, terrible cracking of her soul could be a clean break. "I'm telling the truth. I mean, sneaking into each other's apartments to screw is one thing. But could you imagine taking me to your parents' house for one of their fancy dinner parties?" She laughed, the sound of it brittle and harsh, the jagged edges of it scraping her throat raw. "Picture you, a Sutherland, escorting the poor housekeeper's daughter to—"

"Shut the fuck up."

The enraged snarl burned her ear seconds before hard, implacable fingers clamped down on her arms and whirled her around with enough force to steal the breath from her lungs. Her heart rammed up against her sternum, but not with fear. Need. Lust. It flared to greedy life at his touch, her pussy already softening and clenching in anticipation of having him tunneling through her flesh once more. She whimpered as his mouth slammed down over hers. Helpless, she opened under the relentless carnal onslaught, submitting, silently begging for more. God, the taste of him. Crisp but sultry, like lightning striking wet earth in the midst of a thunderstorm. He electrified her, stunned her. Set her on fire.

She clawed at his shoulders, rising up on tiptoes to increase the almost bruising pressure. *More, more, more*, the sexual creature he'd brought to life inside her chanted. And maybe he heard her. Or possibly, after teaching her the exquisite pleasure he alone could bring her, he just knew what she desired, what she craved. Twisting her hair in a firm, merciless grip, he jerked her head farther back, tilted her face so he could deepen the penetration and angle of his tongue. Mimicking what he would do with her body. Take. Own.

Leave.

*Jesus Christ. What am I doing?*

She wrenched her mouth away from his, and flattening her palms against his shoulders, shoved. Desperation, pain and grief lent her the strength his kiss had robbed from her. Chest heaving, she stumbled past him and lurched for her bed, a rough sob ripping free.

*I can't... I can't...*

"Hayden..." Griffin rasped.

"No!" Wrapping her arms around herself, she shook her head, sinking to the mattress that only minutes ago had been warm and musky with their lovemaking. Now the tangled sheets mocked her naïveté, her foolish dreams of happily ever after with this man. "No," she repeated, squeezing her eyes shut against the sting of moisture. A few minutes. That's all she needed. Then he would be gone, and she could drown in the tears. Just a few more minutes. "You've had your one-for-the-road fuck. Go."

"Baby," he whispered, brushing his fingertips over her jaw.

And for a moment, she trembled under the caress. For a moment, allowed herself to believe she meant something to him.

She was an idiot.

A masochistic idiot.

"Don't call me that. Don't ever call me that again," she said, voice cracking. Dammit, the tears. One escaped and rolled down her cheek. "Get out."

His hand fell from her face, but for a long beat of time, he didn't move. His warm, solid presence reached out to her like a damn tease, taunting her with what she couldn't have. Just as she parted her lips to scream at him to get the fuck out, he shifted, taking his heat with him.

She didn't open her eyes. Not when she heard the rustle of his clothes as he finished dressing. Not when the bedroom door creaked open. Not when the echo of heavy footsteps disappeared.

Not when she curled up on the sheets where his scent still lingered.

Not when the sobs tore free, leaving a hole inside her that would never be filled again.

# CHAPTER TWO

*Five years later*

*A naked blonde walks into a bar with a poodle under one arm and a two-foot salami under the other...*

Hayden frowned. What the hell was the rest of that joke?

She lifted the mug of tepid, dark brown beer, sniffed its yeasty scent, and lowered the glass to the scarred table with no small amount of disgust.

Hell, it didn't matter. The joke was funny in *Breakfast Club* when Judd Nelson was crawling through an air vent during Saturday detention. Not so much when she sat in a Florida dive bar that looked like something straight off the set of a biker B-movie. With said bikers eyeing her as if she were either a narc or serving up the same thing as the skinny blonde with the dark roots, double-D cups and denim skirt up to her See You Next Tuesday. And from the frequent trips to the dingy hallway that led to the restrooms, the woman either had a bladder the size of a pea, or she was serving up pussy like Waffle House hash browns.

And the heat. God. She tugged on the collar of her T-shirt, praying for even the tiniest bit of circulation to cool her damp skin.

She lived in Texas so she was accustomed to hot-as-hell, but damn, Florida, with its smothering, almost tropical humidity, was a whole different animal. And with her curls starting to tighten into a big ass mane, she probably resembled one of those animals. Son-of-a-

9

bitch, she'd only been in the Sunshine State for four hours, and she already hated it. If not for the work assignment that had sent her to this little backwater town and bar, she and her afro would be getting the hell outta Dodge.

Or Blackpool, Florida.

Why anyone with brains, ambition, or a need for a damn Big Mac would voluntarily settle in this wrong turn off I-10 stumped the hell out of her. Seriously. Not. One. McDonald's. From the looks of the clientele in this shit hole of a bar they obviously didn't give a damn about a healthy lifestyle. So that meant the town was just as she'd called it when she'd almost driven right past it: Fucked.

And didn't that just sum up the plethora of reasons why she was sitting in this godforsaken bar in this godforsaken town?

She'd earned a Bachelor's in Managerial Studies and an M.B.A. in Finance. At twenty-six years old, she was the personal assistant to one of the most powerful businessmen in the state of Texas—hell, the whole country. Yet, she'd been reduced to a pseudo-bounty hunter for his wayward son.

Not just any son, though.

Griffin Sutherland.

Her first lover. The man she'd once loved with all the passion of a too-stupid-to-live girl. The man who'd broken her heart and walked out on her without a backward glance or a word in five years.

Yep. Fucked.

But that was a lifetime—and an emotional lobotomy—ago.

She wasn't the same gullible, stars-in-her-eyes young girl Griffin had left sobbing in a fetal position on sheets still carrying the scent of Freshly Fucked. A year after stumbling around like a slightly-cleaner-not-as-bloody zombie, she'd gotten her ass in gear. He'd broken her, but out of the pain, she'd forged someone stronger, smarter, and driven. Someone who didn't take anyone's shit. Someone who wouldn't ever be cock-fodder for another man again.

Any love she'd harbored for Griffin Sutherland had been successfully torched and incinerated years ago by his indifference and silence. But, Joshua Sutherland wasn't privy to the history between her and his youngest son. As far as he knew, they'd been chummy during childhood and up until Griffin had abandoned his family five years ago. In his opinion, who better to send on this retrieval trip than a person his son actually liked?

She snorted.

Joshua would've been better off coming himself. Since "the help" hadn't been invited to Audrey Sutherland's—Joshua's wife and Griffin's mother—birthday party several months ago, Hayden hadn't seen Griffin when he'd returned to Houston to attend. Which was a blessing because ripping off his son's balls the first time she laid eyes on him in five years would've probably been just cause for being fired.

Still…she had to suck up her castrating urges. She hadn't failed a task given to her yet by Joshua, and dragging his black sheep son back to the family fold wouldn't be the first. Even if this was literally the last place she would rather be. And that included hell and Disney World on the 4th of July.

Sighing, she glanced up, searching for the waitress. Her beer was starting to not just look like piss but smell like it. Just as she caught the young woman's eye, a big hulk of a man with a black beard that had to break a record for bushiness, a leather vest and a chest full of tattoos winked at her. A shiver of eew skittered over her skin. Even if she did go for the Blackbeard the pirate look, was that a fucking swastika inked on the side of his neck? Apparently, being a member of the master race didn't prevent him from wanting to bone a Latina. Fucker.

A burst of raucous laughter yanked her attention from Blackbeard and almost drowned out the incongruous tinkle of the bell above the bar's entrance. She glanced up as three men stumbled through the doorway, shoving each other and tossing insults back and forth. She scanned their scruffy faces, stained T-shirts and jeans, hope craning its head up…only to drop back down in disgust. Nope. No Sutherland among them. The tip Joshua had received and passed on to her about this being Griffin's favorite watering hole must've been off.

Disgusted, she rose from her table. This was pointless. After four hours of waiting on him to show and being biker bait, she had to face the facts. Griffin probably wasn't showing up here tonight. That meant cruising the tiny town of Blackpool to find him. Oh fucking goody.

Muttering, she reached for her pocket and the cash she'd stashed there. She might have lived in a cottage on the estate of a million dollar mansion as a child and have resided in the Texas suburbs for the last few years, but Lorena Reynolds hadn't raised a fool. By carrying a purse into this pit, Hayden might as well loop a sign around her neck that declared "Beat the Shit Out of Me and Steal My Money" in red, bold, 48 point font.

"You boys enjoy. Drinks on me tonight."

She froze. That drawl. Slow, thick, and warm like the dark gold, heavy Karo syrup her mother used to pour over pan-fried cornbread when Hayden was younger. Delicious. Pure sin. And familiar. Too damn familiar.

Her ass dropped back to the stool as her heart kicked into a dull, ponderous thud in her chest. It'd been five years since she'd heard that voice. Since then it had teased her, whispered to her...seduced her.

*"Open up for me, baby. That's it. Let me fuck that pretty mouth."*

*"This tight pussy is mine. Mine. Say it."*

*"I could fucking die in you, baby."*

She blinked, beating back the memories that molasses-and-sex voice stirred, locking them away in the vault they'd somehow escaped from. Swallowing past the fist in her throat, she slowly rotated in the direction of the bar.

Wide shoulders and a broad chest tested the fortitude and determination of a plaid shirt stretched over a white T-shirt. Long, thick, muscular thighs encased in sturdy but worn denim. She could only catch a glimpse of his profile, but that small look revealed a man bigger, more muscled than the one in her memories. The formerly short blonde waves were now caught up in one of those pretty-boy man buns. Sure, this area of Florida could probably claim more than one Viking among its population, but only one man had ever incited the *oh shit* dip in her belly. Or that damn lick of heat in her veins.

Griffin.

The man had eviscerated her soul to the point that for a year after he left she hadn't wanted to do anything but lie in a bed and disappear under the covers. Yet, her body still recognized him as the only man who'd ever made it sing like fucking Pavarotti. She'd had one lover since him, and he'd failed in dragging a shattering, damn near mind-bending orgasm out of her like Griffin had. He hadn't made her crave his special brand of lust and passion that had her willing to do anything he asked.

Only Griffin had possessed that power.

God, how she hated him for it.

Hated herself for it.

But that was then. When she'd been a naïve girl eager to please the man on whom she'd believed the sun specifically rose and set. So what her pussy was like Pavlov's pitiful, trained dogs? She didn't want him, didn't need him. And last time she checked, her pussy followed her dictates, not the other way around.

Sliding from the chair once more, she straightened her shoulders, and strode toward the bar. The sooner she delivered her message to the bastard, the sooner she could call this mission accomplished and go home.

The headache-inducing blare of classic rock blaring from the ancient jukebox didn't soften, but damn if it didn't seem as if the volume lowered and every eye zeroed in on her as she cut a path through the tables and stools. Or maybe it was the pounding of her heart. She scoffed. That was ridiculous. What did she have to be afraid of? She'd faced down drunken good-ol'-boys who figured PA meant Piece of Ass. Confronting the man who'd ripped her heart out of her chest and used it for batting practice? Just another day on the job.

Wishing she had a baby wipe to clean the scarred surface of the barstool, she slid onto it.

"Hello, Griffin." Griffin, not Griff. Since they were no longer friends, she didn't have the right, or the inclination, to use the shortened, more intimate version of his name.

The blond giant next to her shifted, a small smile already curving his lips. But she caught the moment recognition entered his eyes, darkening them. That sensual but polite smile fell, leaving an impassive, stoic mask she prayed to God she mimicked.

Silence descended between them, swallowing up the raucous chatter and tinny music. As cliché and trite as it seemed, the world contracted and narrowed until only the two of them remained.

Five years had brought some changes. At twenty-five, Griffin had been leaner, with the hard, beautiful body of a man who spent time in a gym to let off steam. But at thirty, his wide shoulders that blocked out her view of the room behind him, rock solid chest and thick arms put her in the mind of someone who spent less time on a treadmill and more on the sites of his construction company. Those were sweat-and-back-breaking-labor muscles.

But some things had remained the same. The impossibly blue eyes that were all the more brilliant because of his sun-kissed skin and bright hair. The wide, almost-too-full-for-a-man mouth that saved his face, with its chiseled, elegant planes and lines, from verging into pretty boy territory. He still resembled an angel about five minutes after it'd fallen: beautiful and fresh from sinning.

No, she took that back. Now he was more like the huge, powerful, golden mythological creature he'd been named after. A gryphon. Half lion, half eagle. Fierce. Dominant. Stunning in its beauty and just as terrifying.

"Hayden," he murmured, breaking the quiet that had grown deafening with each passing second.

Just that. Not "It's been a long time." Not "How the hell are you?" Or even a "What the fuck are you doing here?" Just her name. She smothered a hard crack of laughter. What had she expected, really? Him to fall out of his chair, delirious with joy to see her? He'd exorcised her out of his life like she hadn't existed. That spoke volumes.

Inhaling a deep breath, she dipped her chin in acknowledgment. "It's good to see you."

He arched a dark brown eyebrow. "Is that right?"

The lie had pretty much scalded her tongue, and from the faint, wry twist of his lips, he'd guessed as much. "I figured it was the polite thing to say."

"Polite." He picked up the brown beer bottle on the bar in front of him, and tipped it to his lips, his hooded gaze remaining fixed on her. "I'd say we're far past manners."

With another sip from his bottle, he slowly scanned her from the top of her by now Fight the Power, afro-thick curls over her white T-shirt and skinny jeans, and down to her stylish wedges that added three inches to her five foot four frame. She fought not to flinch under the slow, thorough perusal that knew every inch of what existed underneath the clothes. And when his scrutiny settled back on her face, she forced herself to meet his hooded stare.

Nothing. No curiosity. No anger. No…heat. Whatever thoughts or feelings at seeing her broiled in his head, they were his own. The Scattered, Smothered, Diced and Peppered whore running a healthy business in the bathroom would've probably received more of a warm welcome.

Damn, it shouldn't sting that her appearance after a five year absence didn't even register on his reaction radar. *She* didn't warrant a reaction.

"I couldn't agree more." She pasted a smile on her mouth that probably resembled Mike Tyson's right before he went for Evander Holyfield's ear. "Your father sent me to find you."

Now that got a reaction. If possible his features hardened further, the chiseled lines appearing to be carved from unforgiving rock. His eyes chilled, the blue freezing to ice chips. A fine tension invaded his body, and as he set his beer on the bar top, the movement was controlled, deliberate. Predatory.

Suddenly, she was very thankful they were in a bar full of people.

"Care to explain that?" he asked. No, the flinty note in his voice demanded.

The pain sucker punched her, catching her right in the chest before she could defend herself. The memory of the last time he'd said those exact words crashed into her, flinging her to the night he'd fucked her then left. She inhaled, breathing past the shards of pain slicing deep. *He doesn't have the power to hurt you anymore. You don't love him.*

"Just what I said. Your father sent me here to find you. I work for him," she said, her voice only slightly husky with the effort of keeping her "Go to hell" scream inside her.

"You work for Joshua," he repeated, anger flickering in his gaze though his voice maintained the bland steadiness she envied. Of course he probably saw her being associated with his father as a big *fuck you*. Like her decisions about her life revolved around him. "Color me surprised. What do you do for my father?"

"I'm his personal assistant." And a damn good one. Joshua Sutherland wasn't known for sentiment, so he hadn't awarded the job to his former housekeeper's daughter out of the kindness of his heart. She'd busted her ass to rise to the position. Working for one of the most successful and wealthiest business men in Texas—a man who was also running for governor—was only the first step in her 10-year career plan.

"Hmm." He propped an elbow on the bar and picking up the bottle again, dangled the neck between his fingers. "You're not his usual type. Or has Joshua given up on the thin, blonde, just old enough to buy alcohol, and with an IQ smaller than their bra size type in the last few years?" He didn't wait for her response, but continued in that same mocking drawl. "I hope so, because, frankly, you're an improvement. Oh, but wait… He fucked the others. Are you fucking Joshua, Hayden?"

The verbal slap stole the breath from her lungs on an agonized gasp. She shot to her feet, almost pitching forward with the sharp momentum. Fuck him. *Fuck. Him.*

She'd taken two steps past him before his hand shot out and wrapped around her wrist. No! The objection shrieked in her head as his skin seemed to brand hers, dragging memories kicking and screaming from the vault of her mind.

Memories of his fingers cuffing her wrists, holding her arms above her head as he pounded inside her with a fierce wildness that marked her pussy and her soul. Of one hand tangled in her hair, holding her steady, while the other fisted his cock, feeding it to her slowly. Of his fingertips pressed into her thighs, spreading her wide for his greedy mouth.

"Let me go," she snarled, jerking at his grasp. "You don't get to judge me. And you damn sure don't get to touch me."

"Sit down," he snapped, his grip unrelenting. When she didn't obey him, his eyes narrowed, and she detested the arrow of lust that pierced her sex. Detested him for making her feel it, remember it. "Sit. Down. Hayden."

Every cell in her body longed to tell him to eff off, but she had a job to do. The sooner she accomplished her task, the sooner she could get the hell away from him for at least another five years.

Sliding back onto the stool, she directed a pointed stare down at his long, hard fingers still manacling her wrist. Several moments passed before he slowly released her. With Herculean effort, she refrained from rubbing the skin that tingled and burned from his touch.

"I'm sorry. That was uncalled for." The harsh planes of his face didn't soften with the apology. "Why are you working for Joshua?"

She didn't owe him an explanation; she didn't owe him shit. Not that she worked for his father as some sort of "Fuck you" to Griffin. That would mean she cared. That he influenced her decisions. And the moment five years ago when her love hadn't affected his, he'd lost that same privilege.

*Take me with you.*

The plea whispered across her mind, the humiliation and pain nipping at its heels. She'd fucking begged him, and he'd still walked out, leaving her to deal with the fallout of giving her heart to someone who didn't see her as worthy enough to stay. To love. So, to hell with him. Whatever decisions she'd made in the last five years to survive, to succeed, to live, he had no say in. He didn't get an opinion.

Instead of answering him, she reached into her back pocket and withdrew the envelope Joshua had given her before she'd headed to Florida.

"Here." She slapped the letter down onto the bar. "This is for you."

He flicked a glance down at it before returning his attention to her. "What is it?"

"I don't know. Your father asked me to deliver it to you. And now that I have," she rose and set down enough money to cover her two beers, "my job is done. Good-bye, Griffin."

This time he didn't stop her. And she was relieved.

She was, dammit.

# CHAPTER THREE

In Griffin Sutherland's years, he'd seen some shit. Dumb shit. Dangerous shit. Perverted shit. Seen it and even participated in a few. But at a jaded thirty years old, none of it had surprised him. None had sent him spinning head over ass like he'd walked into a fist and got knocked the hell out.

Not until Hayden Reynolds had walked up to him at one of his favorite quitting-time bars looking like an unattainable, gorgeous queen in a place packed with bikers, construction workers, drunks and whores.

He inhaled, willing his cock to calm the hell down as watched Hayden forge a path through the tables and thickening crowd toward the bar's entrance. But when he sucked in a whiff of the sultry perfume she'd left behind—the perfume that reminded him of vanilla, honey and sex—his dick rebelled, hardening to the point of pain. Too bad he couldn't put the motherfucker in time-out like the disobedient kid it resembled.

Hayden.

Damn.

The sight of her had been a knee to the balls. Shocking. Painful. Leaving behind an ache that hadn't ebbed yet.

Jesus Christ, she was stunning. Sexy. Fuckable. So goddamn fuckable.

How many shades of asshole did it make him that even as she'd stared at him with disgust darkening her pretty hazel eyes all he could

18

think about was if her pussy would still strangle him in its two-sizes-too-small and just perfect grip?

He closed his eyes, grinding his molars together so hard, a cloud of white dust should've puffed from his nose. The years hadn't diminished his memory. Without any effort at all he could feel her slick, molten heat clutching his cock, quivering around him in orgasm. Could hear the wet suction of her flesh welcoming and releasing him as he fucked into her like a damn madman. Could taste the tangy sheen of sweat that had glistened on her skin.

Could see the devastation and betrayal on her face as he'd told her he was leaving Texas. Leaving her.

"Shit," he growled under his breath, curling his fingers around his beer in a death grip. She hadn't understood why he'd had to escape the stifling rule of his father and the Sutherland name then, and from the cold, go-to-hell-in-gasoline-drawers vibe she'd emanated moments ago, she still didn't get it. And she also wouldn't comprehend that he didn't regret his decisions.

In the handful of years since, he'd founded a construction company that now employed fifty men and contracted many more. They had earned a reputation of quality, efficient work in the tri-state area, and the company continued to steadily grow. Where most start-up businesses had to close their doors after the first two years, Griffin's was turning a healthy profit.

He'd done this. With the help of his grandfather and grandmother's seed money they hadn't allowed him to refuse—and that he'd paid back two years ago—he'd achieved his goal of becoming his own man, of establishing something that was a product of his own vision and hard work.

Still... Walking out of her bedroom and apartment that night had damn near killed him. When she'd asked to go with him, he'd almost said yes. Almost given in just to have her close to him. But that would've been selfish. Deciding to quit his cushy job at his father's company, leaving his family—especially his sister and grandfather—and moving clear across the country to do God-knew-what had been selfish enough. He couldn't add interrupting Hayden's college education and stealing her chance at a stable, certain future to the list, too.

For him, it'd been his one altruistic act.

But she'd seen it as a rejection. Of her. Of their fourteen year-long friendship. Of the relationship they'd shared those last eight months.

Once more an image of her face in that shadowed bedroom wavered across his mind. And he compared it to the face of the woman who'd sat across from him seconds earlier. Still the loveliest blend of green, brown and gold eyes he'd ever seen. Still framed by the thickest, longest lashes. Back then, her eyes had been filled with confusion, hurt and love.

Tonight, when loathing hadn't shadowed her gaze, there'd been indifference.

The indifference had scored a burning path across his chest more than the hatred. The latter meant she at least felt something toward him. But the cool disinterest? It told him she couldn't give a shit. He was nothing. Forgotten. Meaningless.

Not that he'd ever forgotten her. That would be like Dorothy forgetting she'd been caught up in a twister and transported to another land that had forever changed her life. Hayden had been—was—his cyclone, his Oz.

Lifting his beer, he took a deep sip, and when he lowered the bottle back to the bar, his fingers nudged the envelope she'd left behind. His name typed across the front snagged his attention. Snorting, he couldn't contain his small sneer. Hayden had said the letter was from his father. Joshua hadn't even bothered to write his own son's name on the piece of mail. Probably had one of his flavor of the month secretaries do it.

Dismissing it, he leaned forward on his stool, narrowing his eyes on her.

At least she hadn't tamed those curls. He'd loved the wild mane, enjoyed tangling his fingers in the heavy silk. The strands had been a sensory delight when they'd caressed his palms, chest...thighs. The young woman he'd known might have traded in her colorful tight tank tops and sweaters and flowing skirts for a more conservative shirt and jeans, but the free, riotous spirals and waves telegraphed the passionate, sexual creature he remembered still existed.

Not that the conservative didn't look hot on her. With those gorgeous, more-than-a-handful breasts and fuck me curves, she would transform a burlap sack into something Victoria's Secret worthy. And that ass. He lowered his gaze to the flesh filling out the tight denim. Swallowed down a groan on a mouthful of alcohol.

He'd had that ass. Had been the first man to slide his dick

between those perfect cheeks and penetrate the tiny hole and tight-as-a-fist channel. Had been the first to stretch it, fuck it.

With a cursory scan around the room, he caught more than a few men staring, probably imagining what he'd already had.

Fuckers.

Slamming the bottle onto the bar, he surged from his stool and strode after her. The hell was she thinking coming into this dive looking pristine and untouchable? Didn't she know that made men want to touch?

But damn if they would. Not her. She was off limits. From them.

And from him.

Just as he reached her, one asshole stretched a hand toward her, his fingertips almost brushing her arm. Griffin scowled at him, and the guy dropped his arm, but not his eyes. Maybe if Griffin blackened them for staring at what was his...

What. The. Fuck.

Where had that thought come from? Well, he knew where—straight from his mad-as-hell dick. But she wasn't his. Not anymore. Not ever again.

So much water under that damn bridge he would need an ark to cross it.

He pressed his palm to her lower back, clenching his jaw at the stiffening of her spine. "Deal with it," he murmured in her ear. "Every bastard in this place is staring at your ass like it's on the fucking menu. I'm not letting you walk out of here or to your car alone."

Wonder of all wonders, she didn't shove his hand away or tell him what to do with his offer. Moments later, they exited the bar into the stifling June night, the humidity settling on his shoulders like a damp, smothering blanket. After half a decade, he should've been used to the tropical-like heat, yet sometimes the weather still seemed like a Viking's sauna. And tonight, with the unwanted throb of lust adding its own blaze, he was tempted to strip.

"Did you read the letter?"

Griffin glanced down at Hayden, but her attention was riveted straight ahead at the parking lot littered with pick-up trucks, motorcycles and a mish-mash of older model vehicles. A far cry from the expensive, sleek, immaculate vehicles that had occupied the well-kept grounds of the Texas country club he'd frequented years ago.

The world Hayden now belonged to even peripherally if she worked for his father.

A bolt of anger flashed through him at the reminder of her employer. As irrational as the sense of betrayal that had lanced him at her announcement was, he couldn't stifle it. Two people had been privy to his bitterness and resentment toward Joshua Sutherland: Bud Sutherland, Griffin's grandfather, and Hayden. To the public, Griffin had been the privileged second son who had been granted a position in the vast conglomerate of Sutherland Industries by his generous father. But the truth had been far different. No love was lost between father and son.

And Hayden had been aware of it. Yet, she'd gone to work for the very man who'd made Griffin's life a living hell.

"No." He dropped his hand from her back. "I don't need to since I'm not interested in anything Joshua has to say."

"He's running for governor, you know."

No, he hadn't known. And didn't care.

"I send my condolences to the people of Texas if he makes it into office. It'll probably become a police state under his tender mercies. Wait, is that why—" He grasped her arm, and she flinched away from him. Anger and something else—something that left a bruise in his chest—flared inside him. "Does my touch offend you that much? I'm not going to attack you, Hayden," he snapped.

"Yes, it does offend me. I pick and choose who puts their hands on me, and you're not even on the short list."

The sharp retort jabbed at him, landing a blow he couldn't ignore. Not questioning the urge to push her, to make her eat those words, he crowded into her personal space. Didn't stop until his chest was a breath away from grazing the tips of those beautiful breasts.

"I used to be," he reminded her, voice as hard as his dick. "I used to be the only one on the list."

"That was a long time ago."

"Not long enough to forget, though, right?" He cocked his head to the side, peered down into her face. Caught the flicker in her eyes. "No, you haven't forgotten, have you, Hayden?" he whispered against her ear. Soft, thick curls grazed his cheek, and he subtly inhaled their apple-scented fragrance. The same one she'd used before. "Who's at the top of the list now? Some uptight, junior executive from Joshua's office? Some safe, boring *gentleman*," he sneered, "who needs a map to your pussy, and then a manual on how to get you off once he finds it? Some prude who thinks two minutes in the missionary position is good fucking? He doesn't know how hard and messy you like it, does he, baby? He doesn't know how you love your pussy eaten then fucked? How you love a dick thrusting between those gorgeous tits. He doesn't know how much you scream when a cock is sliding into your sweet, tight ass." He chuckled, the sound rough, serrated even to his ears. "No, he doesn't know any of that."

Their harsh breaths filled the heavy silence in the parking lot, the raucous din from the bar not reaching them. The quick puffs escaping her parted lips bathed the base of his throat, and he craved them on his mouth. His cock. He curled his fingers into fists, tightening them until the skin across his knuckles protested. He damn sure hadn't been a monk since they'd separated. But every fuck had been in an effort to forget her, deny the hunger that could only be satisfied by her. An attempt to search for serenity after the fury of sex had quieted. And each attempt had failed. Miserably.

Because none of them had been Hayden.

No woman had ever turned him into the Human Torch with just her scent, with a look, with just a gasp of air across his T-shirt covered chest. Only Hayden possessed that superpower.

"Don't pretend you have any idea about who I am. Or about what I need or want." She shifted back a step, and when her head tilted back, the aloof mask was firmly in place. "Who or how I fuck isn't any of your business. As a matter-of-fact, my business is done here. You have the letter. Read it, don't read it. As I said before, I was supposed to hunt you down and deliver it regardless of how distasteful I found the errand. Mission accomplished. Good-bye, Griffin."

She wound her way through the cars, and after unlocking the door of a black Nissan, slid into the car and drove off. He remained standing in the dark long after the red of her headlights disappeared.

*Don't pretend you have any idea about who I am. Or about what I need or want.*

She was right. He didn't know the woman she'd become. The reserved, cold one who'd basically told him to fuck off. The girl he'd held, teased, confided in during the darkest hours of night had been open, giving, lighthearted...trusting. This woman didn't look like she laughed often. And damn sure didn't trust easily. What had happened in the time since he'd last seen her? And had he been responsible?

A vicious knot tightened his gut.

Not able—or willing—to dwell on that last question, he pivoted and headed back to the bar. To the life he'd chosen over the one he'd left. To the people who'd earned the label of family more than the one to whom he'd been born.

"Everything okay, Griff?" Jessie Montgomery, his foreman and best friend, clapped Griffin on the shoulder as he reclaimed the seat he'd abandoned earlier.

"Yeah." He reached for his beer, but at the last moment, pushed it across the bar. "Just an old," he paused, "acquaintance."

"A fine as hell one, too." Jessie flicked a hand at the bartender, gesturing toward Griffin. In seconds, another brew appeared in front of him, along with a sly smile. At any other time, he might have considered taking up the sexy brunette on the offer in that grin. But not tonight. Not when vanilla, honey and sex still invaded his nostrils. "I can't believe you came back in here alone. Or at all."

Griffin grunted, not willing to talk about Hayden, not even to Jessie.

His friend shrugged and slid a white envelope under Griffin's elbow. The envelope that had been Hayden's "business" in Florida.

"I wasn't sure if you were returning, so I grabbed this for you. It has your name on it."

For a moment, Griffin just stared at the piece of mail as if it contained Ebola. He probably wasn't far off. Anything that came from his father would be laced with a poison that attacked his confidence, peace or pride.

Still, something had him picking up the letter. Morbid curiosity. The messenger.

Before he could reconsider, Griffin ripped the end of the envelope and removed two sheets of paper. Again, typed. He snorted.

But two minutes later, all hints of amusement evaporated. Replaced by shock. And rage. A black, blazing rage. He slid the letter behind the second sheet. A deed.

That son-of-a-bitch.

# CHAPTER FOUR

"Excuse me, sir, do you have an appointment?" The thin blonde scurried around her receptionist desk, alarm widening her eyes and hiking her voice to a decibel just under for-dogs'-hearing-only. "Sir, you can't just walk in there—"

"Don't worry." Griffin waved his hand toward her desk, tossing her a grin that felt feral. "He's expecting me."

It'd been a week since he'd read the letter Hayden had delivered from his father. Yeah, Joshua Sutherland knew Griffin would come to Houston, Texas. To him.

He'd probably counted on it.

Griffin opened the closed door to his father's office and strode in, shutting the door behind him, and locking the yipping receptionist out.

Joshua glanced up from his desk, his expression stoic and not betraying an ounce of surprise. He didn't rise from his chair to greet Griffin, but reclined against the back, linking his fingers over his still-flat stomach. At 54, his father seemed to have avoided the touch of time. Except for a light sprinkling of gray in his otherwise thick, dark hair, he seemed as young, fit and strong as he'd been since Griffin's childhood. His dark eyes remained clear and assessing. Yes, Griffin could easily imagine his good looks and imposing presence easily swaying the good people of Texas to vote him in as their next governor. Like sheep ushering in the wolf to their pasture.

"Griffin."

"Joshua."

Aside from the slight tightening of his mouth, his father didn't respond to Griffin's refusal to call him Dad or Father. Griffin hadn't used either word when addressing his father in six years. Not since the night he'd entered his father's office and found his girlfriend riding Joshua like a jockey at the Kentucky Derby. Catching one's father fucking the woman who was supposed to be yours didn't exactly foster warm, familial feelings.

"Sorry for showing up unannounced," Griffin crossed the office and dropped into the visitor's chair in front of the massive, glass desk that dominated the cavernous office. "But as I told your secretary, I'm sure my presence here isn't a surprise. As a matter of fact, I'm sure you knew the moment I entered the building."

"That's still no excuse for your rudeness to my staff, Griffin." His eyebrows arched on the tail end of the patronizing admonishment. "With such a melodramatic entrance, I'm assuming you're here about my letter."

"You're damn right I am," Griffin snapped. Reaching into the inner pocket of his jacket, he rose, withdrew the copy of the deed and slapped it onto the desk. "Why?"

He didn't need to elaborate. Joshua would know exactly to what he referred. His father's legal claim on the property that Griffin had been negotiating to purchase for three months. The parcel of land behind a hospital in Florida that Joshua shouldn't know about. And since the piece of property wasn't large enough to build a high-rise or shopping outlet on, Joshua shouldn't have any interest in it. But the deed with Joshua's name on it rejected that belief. His father had somehow swooped in and stolen the land out from under Griffin.

Rage that hadn't abated since he'd first opened the envelope and read the summons to return home, swirled in his chest like a tornado gaining power and strength with each rotation. A power play. He recognized it. Had witnessed Joshua employing it on his business opponents. Now he'd used it against him—his own son.

"It's business, Griffin. Not personal." His father tsked, the corner of his mouth curling into a slight sneer. "No wonder your," a pause, "*company* hasn't maximized its potential if you can't separate the two."

"Bullshit." He narrowed his eyes, not betraying the bright flash of pain Joshua's jab at not just Griffin's business, but his ability to run it caused to radiate in his chest. "This is as personal as it gets. Somehow you found out I was bidding on this land, and then decided to buy it out from under me." The deed revealed Joshua had paid twenty-five thousand dollars more than Griffin's offer to the seller. Fifteen thousand more than what the land appraised for. "I've never known you to make a deal that didn't benefit you in some way. And after a week of pondering what you could possibly want with a piece of land behind a regional hospital in the middle of Bumfuck, Florida and coming up with nothing, your reason must have something to do with me. So what do you want, Joshua? Enlighten me so I can tell you to fuck off, and we can go back to our normal habit of pretending the other doesn't exist."

"Watch your mouth, boy," Joshua growled, slowly standing, a muscle jumping along his jaw. "I'm still your father, and you will give me respect."

Griffin snorted. *Like hell*. Respect was earned not commanded. And his father had lost his long ago. Aside from the very rare family obligation that dragged him to Houston, like his mother's birthday celebration a few months back, he made it his personal ambition and goal to maintain at least a three-state distance between him and his father. They'd never gotten along. Even when Griffin had been a child, it'd been his older brother and "Irish twin", Josh, who'd garnered Joshua's attention. Griffin, the "spare" to Josh's "heir", had been an afterthought in birth and affection. Not to mention, Josh was their father's mini-me in appearance and personality. Father and son drew people to them with their affability, flawless mannerisms and perfection. While Griffin, the only blonde haired and blue-eyed child, with his wildness, brooding and tendency to offend with his blunt honesty, had differed from his father and brother in everything but stubbornness. In that trait, they were identical.

Joshua had barely tolerated Griffin, and Griffin—desperate for his father's approval and regard, but always hurt by seeming to fall short—had lived by the motto that any attention, even negative, was good attention.

Until the moment when he'd interrupted Joshua screwing his girlfriend, and Griffin just stopped giving a fuck.

The betrayal hadn't been about the girl; at twenty-four, she'd been the latest in a long line of "latests." It hadn't even been about his father's lack of fidelity to his wife, Griffin's mother. Joshua's affairs had been an ill-kept secret in their family—as in not a secret at all.

But Griffin's mother, Audrey, turned a blind eye to her husband's infidelity and would never leave him, so Griffin had pretended to ignore them as well.

No, the pain, disillusionment and rage had been about his father's lack of loyalty. His utter disregard for his own son's hurt. Joshua's countless sermons about the honor of being a Sutherland, about integrity and allegiance to family... It'd all been reduced to sugar-coated shit.

"That ship not only sailed, it was torpedoed and blown to hell and back." Curling his lip in a derisive sneer, he leaned forward, his palms planted on the top of his father's desk. "Now, how about we just discuss why you requested my presence. Because we both know that's all this is." He flicked the deed across the glass. "A way of getting me to come to Houston on your terms."

"You're wrong, Griffin." The annoyed frown cleared from his father's face, a calm, detached note entering his voice. Both sowed a kernel of dread in Griffin's gut. "That property is beneficial to me. The hospital would eagerly pay me a monthly leasing fee if I cleared the land and turned it into a parking lot. Guaranteed profit for me and convenience for them. Win-win."

With Herculean effort, Griffin schooled his features to reveal nothing. Not the panic that sizzled through him. Or the fury that clawed at him like a caged beast. Both would betray the importance of the land to Joshua. And only a fool would expose his vulnerable underbelly to a predator.

"Or..."

"Now we're getting down to it," Griffin drawled. "Or what, Joshua? What do you want?"

"Or you can agree to stay in Houston for the next month, and at the end of that time, I will deed the property over to you."

"And if I don't?"

His father cocked his head to the side, his dark gaze unflinching. Unrepentant. "Then I pave it over into a parking lot, contact the hospital and negotiate with them."

A crimson haze hijacked his vision, a fist of suffocating rage tightening around his throat. For several seconds, he didn't reply, attempting to rein in his anger. Or at least not let his father glimpse it. "Blackmail?" He arched an eyebrow. "That's a new low even for you."

"Bargaining," Joshua corrected. "I have something you want, and you have something I need in return. How badly do you want this property?"

Badly. But damn if Griffin would ever admit that to him.

"Not enough to abandon my company and the people who depend on me for a month. You might think my business is second rate, but it's mine. And I'm not going to be away from it for that long."

A scowl darkened his father's face. "You belong here, working with your family, not playing across the country. I've given you plenty of time to come to that realization yourself."

"You've given me nothing. I've earned and worked hard for everything I have, and didn't ask you for anything. And that's what sticks in your craw, doesn't it, Joshua? You thought I would come crawling back to you within a year." He straightened, balled his fingers into fists next to his thighs. "What is it that you need? If you wanted me to come home more often, all you had to do was ask." His father didn't want him home any more than Griffin wanted to be there. The telephone worked both ways, and in the years Griffin had been gone, Joshua hadn't dialed once.

"I'm running for governor, and though the election isn't until November—five months from now—we've already started solidifying my platform, image and branding. Several informal polls have indicated family values is one of the most important concerns for voters. They want a governor who has strong morals—"

Griffin snorted.

"—is Christian and supports and exhibits the traditional, American family," Joshua finished with a glare. "We have several important events planned in the next month, and I need my family to attend them."

"So you want to dupe the people of Texas into believing the Sutherlands are one big, happy, loving family." He shook his head. "This is fucking ridiculous. You're blackmailing me into staying here so you can lie to the same people who would vote you into office."

"Grow up, Griffin," Joshua snapped, slashes of red staining his cheekbones.

"That's what I left five years ago to do. Now I'm going to get back to it." Pivoting on his heel, he stalked toward the door. "Run your con game with someone else."

"This offer stands until midnight tonight. This time tomorrow morning, I will be contacting the hospital."

"Do what you have to do, Joshua." Griffin twisted the knob and strode out of the office, fury like jet fuel, propelling him forward and out of the downtown Houston glass monolith that housed the offices of Sutherland Industries.

As he hit the sidewalk, his cell phone vibrated in his pants pocket. For a moment, he almost ignored it. But at the third ring, he removed it with a soft curse. His stomach clenched before dipping at the name that scrolled across the screen. Quickly, he swiped the 'answer' bar and pressed the phone to his ear.

"Hello."

"Hi, Griff." The high-pitched, girlish voice echoed in his ear. And though he smiled, the jagged edges of panic didn't soften.

"Hey, lady bug." He closed his eyes and the image of Sarah, the lovely eight year-old girl with the wide brown eyes, pixie features and smooth, bald head flickered across his mind. "How're you doing?"

"Fine. Mommy's in the cafeteria for coffee, but I took her phone when she wasn't looking."

Griffin laughed, easily imagining Sarah's impish grin. "That's my little thief. Although now I'm wondering if I should've let you watch Oliver Twist. You seemed to have picked up some bad habits."

"I'm going to be in a musical when I grow up. I'm going to be the first girl to play the Artful Dodger on Broadway."

*When I grow up.* Her proclamation punched him in the chest, leaving a terrible, throbbing ache behind. Opening his eyes, he stared across the street. Only he didn't see the SunTrust branch but Sarah, with needles and tubes in her arms where the chemotherapy drugs streamed into her little body. Sarah, with her bright pink and purple scarves wrapped around her head, her indomitable spirit not marred by the acute lymphocytic leukemia attacking her system. Sarah, soldiering through the vomiting, the mouth sores and listlessness that plagued her as a result of the disease.

Griffin had met the little girl five years ago when he hired her father, Jessie. He'd become close with the tough, native Floridian and his pretty, shy wife Mary Ann. And their cherubic daughter, Sarah, three years old at the time, had stolen his heart. Griffin loved the little girl as if she were his own niece, just as he considered her father his brother-by-choice. When she'd been diagnosed with cancer a year ago, he'd been by her and her parents' side. He'd rejoiced when she'd entered remission—and cried when a month ago, the disease had returned. For the past three weeks, Sarah had been in the hospital receiving an aggressive chemotherapy treatment. The drugs took their toll, yet Sarah remained cheerful, hopeful and a beacon of light to the adults who loved her.

"I plan to be in the front row. Make sure in your interviews, you tell everyone if not for me, you wouldn't have had your start."

She giggled. "Deal."

"Good." His smile faded. "How're you feeling, lady bug?"

Sarah's soft sigh squeezed his heart in a punishing fist. "Okay. Just tired." A heavy pause. "I heard Mommy crying last night when she thought I was asleep. She thinks I'm going to die," the little girl whispered.

"No, she doesn't," Griffin quickly assured her, detesting hearing the word 'die' coming from her. It seemed blasphemous she even thought the word much less spoke it. Sarah should be running around a playground, singing, dancing, hanging with her friends like other eight year olds. Not lying in a hospital bed listening to her mother weep in the dead of night. "She's just worried about you, sweetheart. She's your mom, so it hurts her that you're sick and hurting. That's all. We all know you're going to kick this. And as soon as the doctors okay it, I'm taking you to New York so we can see Wicked." He'd bought Sarah the soundtrack, and the little girl loved it, and talked frequently about wanting to see the play.

"You promise?"

"Cross my heart." He sketched the symbol over his heart even though she couldn't see the gesture.

"Okay. When are you coming to see me?"

Cursing his father for taking him away from the little girl who needed him, Griffin tightened his grip around the cell. "I had to come home to Texas for a few days," he explained, his tone revealing none of the anger swirling inside him. "But I'll be back soon."

"Good," she chirped. "I was looking out my window this morning. When are you going to build my playground, Griff? I can't wait to see it."

Again, rage ripped through him. Sarah's playground. The one he planned to construct on the land his father now owned and had designated for a parking lot. Damn him. To Joshua, the property was a bargaining chip. To Griffin, it was a promise he'd made the first time Sarah had been sick. The property had become available three months ago, and Griffin had jumped at the opportunity to buy it and grant an oasis of joy to children like Sarah where they could forget the disease that ravaged their bodies. Even for those who weren't well enough to zip down the slides or soar for the sky on the swings, they could look out on it and hope and dream for the day they could. That land was his gift to Sarah and all those children.

And Joshua had stolen it with no thought but to his own wants and end game.

Not that his father's schemes and machinations or Griffin's pride mattered when it came to Sarah. None of it did.

"I'm still working on it, lady bug. But I promise you're going to have your playground. Have I ever broken a promise to you?"

"Nope, never." Her delighted laughter tripped down the line. "Are you going to bring me a gift?"

Griffin chuckled, shaking his head. "You got it. What do you want?"

"A Dallas Cheerleader Barbie!"

"Of course you do," he drawled. It looked like he would be making a trip to the toy store.

"Ooh, Mommy's coming. I'll call you back."

"All right, sweetheart. Now don't get caught trying to sneak the phone back into her purse."

"Of course not! I'm the Artful Dodger! Bye," she whispered, and the call ended.

Still laughing with Sarah's happy voice echoing in his head, Griffin tucked the cell back in his pants pocket. And sighed.

Dragging a hand over his head, he turned and headed back into the building behind him.

He had some negotiating to do.

# CHAPTER FIVE

Hayden slammed her car door shut, taking a petty satisfaction in the loud bang. Since she couldn't yell, cuss and kick something—or somebody—slamming her door would have to suffice. For now. The morning was still young.

Especially since for the next two weeks she would be the personal assistant to one Griffin Sutherland.

Oh yes, a lot of slamming doors and cursing was in her immediate future.

Hiking her bag strap over her shoulder, she inhaled and stared at the townhome with the detached garage before her. Beautiful. But set in the exclusive and moneyed Memorial area of Houston, its attractiveness wasn't surprising. Brick and two stories with a perfectly manicured, small lawn. Except for the cheerful chirping of birds, the serene setting was quiet, homey even.

How would the good people of this neighborhood react if they knew the devil had moved into their midst?

Grumbling under her breath, she stomped—hard to do in four inch stilettos, but still doable—up the sidewalk leading to the front door that was tucked into a corner of the house, an overhang providing shade from the broiling Texas sun. She knocked on the door. Waited. Knocked again. Waited some more.

"Are you kidding me?" she muttered, lifting her fist to pound on the wood. Again. "This is ridiculous…"

The door swung open.

"Really, Sunshine. It's barely nine o'clock in the morning. Much too early to be frowning." Griffin arched an eyebrow. "Especially before coffee." He pivoted and disappeared inside the house.

She tried to utter a comeback. It sat right on the tip of her tongue. Unfortunately, said tongue was currently glued to the roof of her mouth thanks to the miles and miles of golden, taut skin that had filled her vision seconds ago.

God, he was so *big*.

Fuck milk.

These past five years had done a body good.

Her first assumption when she'd seen him in that Florida bar had been right. The kind of strength and muscles he sported weren't earned by countless hours in a gym. No, his hard, sculpted body was probably the product of labor, of time in the sun sweating next to his men. Not one pale line striped his body. Every inch of his chest, shoulders, arms and back were like molten gold. The breath stalled than stuttered in her lungs.

He was beautiful.

Before he'd left, she'd always compared him to a god, one of the regal and impossibly gorgeous Greek Parthenon she'd loved to read about. Now he was...*more*. So much more. Powerful. Intimidating even. A flutter tickled her belly, arrowing in a sinuous glide south until that same whisper of sensation teased her sex. Hell, it'd been so long since she'd felt a tickle, flutter or tease down there. Why did it have to be this man who had to remind her that her pussy still worked?

*Move.* She glanced down at her feet, glaring at the peep toes of her nude shoes. *Move, damn it.* Good Lord, if he turned around and caught her ogling him like a damn peeper... Mortified wouldn't begin to describe the shame. The humiliation. She was over him. Didn't want him. Her pussy might've picked this moment to exhibit signs of life, but that was biology. Like a dieting woman catching sight of red velvet cake. But like that Weight Watchers devotee, she could decide to say no.

And insist he put on a damn shirt.

Forcing herself forward, she entered the home, and shutting the door behind her, pretended like she hadn't just trapped herself in the lion's den wearing Lady Gaga's meat bikini. A very nice den. High ceilings, flawless wood floors, an open, airy floor plan, floor-to-ceiling windows that granted a view of the woodsy area in the back, and a curving staircase that led to an upper level. She thought of her perfectly lovely two bedroom, one bath condo and smothered the sting of apartment-envy.

"Coffee?" Griffin asked from the spacious kitchen with its multitude of pale wood cabinets, a stove that would make Chef Emeril weep in thanksgiving and a huge, freestanding, butcher block island.

"No, thank you."

He shrugged, the muscles under his skin doing a sensual flex and shift. When he turned, she tried to drag her gaze from him. Really tried. But like the man embodied some kind of magnetic pull, she stared at the wide expanse of his shoulders, down the shallow indent of his spine to the narrow span of his waist. And lower. Positively indecent the way the pair of black sweatpants clung to his hips. Even more so because she remembered clearly what the cotton hid.

Hard flesh perfect for digging her fingernails—or heels—into. And she'd done both. She'd also clutched those shoulders, clawed his back, and in the quiet, in the peace after the carnal storm, she'd rested her head on that chest.

When he'd brushed the blunt tips of his long, elegant fingers down her spine, up her nape and into her hair, she'd felt desired, cherished...loved.

But it'd been a lie. The naïve *girl* she'd been had perceived every touch, kiss, and stroke as love when it'd only been sex. Hot, erotic, dirty sex that could be easily gotten and walked away from.

And he hadn't hesitated to do exactly that.

The reminder banished the onslaught of memories, leaving her encased in ice. Best she remember not just who stood across from her, but what he'd left behind him: a broken, grieving mess.

Never would she return to that black, vulnerable place. Never would she allow anyone to reduce her to that agony-filled, needy creature again. A creature so dependent on a man and his imagined love, she couldn't think, couldn't function. No one would ever again be so important to her that she'd lose herself.

That wasn't love. It was craziness.

"Frankly, I'm surprised you're here. I thought you weren't interested in what your father had to say. And yet, here you are." She splayed her hands wide, the gesture encompassing the townhome.

He glanced over his shoulder, his blue eyes shuttered. "You don't know why I'm here?"

"I'm your father's personal assistant, not his Mother Confessor."

"So he just states an order, and you carry it out, no questions." He turned back to finish brewing his coffee in the single-cup coffeemaker, his tone devoid of emotion. Still, she caught the accusation and censure in the question that was a statement. And bristled at it.

"It's my job," she snapped.

"Right. Your job. No matter who your employer uses or what underhanded, questionable tactics he engages, it's your job. I wonder where that line is for you, Hayden. Or if there is one."

"Your issues with your father aren't mine." There'd once been a time when they would've been, when his enemies would've been hers. When those who'd sought to hurt him would've had to come through her first. But that was before he'd left her weeping and shattered in a dark bedroom. "He's never been anything but professional with me."

Facing her, cup in hand, he leaned a hip against the counter. Snorted. "He's Joshua Sutherland. Shame on you if you let your hatred for me blind you to that fact."

Heat poured into her face. "Did it not occur to you that my choices for my life might not revolve around you? They haven't for five years. The last decision was when I begged you to take me with you." Oh *fuck*. Why had she allowed that last, *telling* part slip?

The ice in his eyes melted a fraction, his full lips softening from its grim line. "Hayden..."

"No." She shook her head. "I'm not going there with you. *We're* not going there. Ever. Now," she drew in a breath, crossed her arms, not caring if it betrayed the vulnerability racing through her, "why are you here, and why have I been passed around like chattel?"

His gaze narrowed on her, his body going as still as a statue. The sensual curves of his mouth flattened once more, and she braced herself. Maybe he didn't intend to heed her warning and pursue the line of conversation she refused to discuss. Travelling that pitted road into the past would only lead to pain. His.

Several seconds passed before he lifted his mug and sipped, studying her over the rim.

"I'm here because my father stole a piece of land I wanted from under me so he could blackmail me. If I want him to sell it to me, I have to remain in Houston for the next two weeks." He bit the explanation out, every word coated in a red shade of bitter. As she struggled to digest the information, he continued. "You're here, because if I have to suffer, than you're going to be sitting right beside me in this hell. Be thankful. He originally demanded a month, but I bargained him down to a couple of weeks."

"You don't find that petty and oh, I don't know, childish?" She advanced a step, gripping the edge of the granite bar that separated the kitchen from the living and dining areas. "It didn't even register that this stunt is messing with my job?"

She hadn't taken two consecutive weeks off since she'd started working for Joshua two years ago. She couldn't afford to. Not when others would leap at the chance to occupy her position as the PA for a Sutherland. An image of her temporary replacement flittered across her mind's eye. Young, skinny, pretty, blonde. And ambitious. No doubt she would use the next fourteen days to ingratiate herself to her employer. Knowing Joshua's penchant for her type, the thought was more than a little frustrating…and panicking.

She'd worked her ass off to obtain this position and keep it. Working for Griffin's father was just a step toward her ultimate dream and goal: founding and owning her own financial consultant and management firm. In her ten year goal, she would have enough capital, experience and connections to work for herself, dependent on no one. Be able to provide for her mother so she didn't have to clean house for one more wealthy family a day in her life.

But Griffin, with his thoughtlessness, had thrown a kink—a potentially massive kink—in her plans.

"My father might have a screwed up moral compass, but he's not an idiot." Griffin arched a dark eyebrow. "Besides, think of this as a mini-vacation. For the next two weeks you don't have to field calls from my mother and lie about Joshua attending 'evening business dinners' when you both know he's out fucking his latest mistress. Or you don't have to worry about getting your jewelry orders straight. Y'know, praying you don't mistakenly send the wife the side-piece's pair of earrings? I'm sure all that deception can really wear on a person. You can thank me later."

The denial hovered on her tongue, but she didn't utter it. Hell yes, the lies and juggling of Joshua's blatant infidelity became tiresome. It was the one aspect of her job she detested. Joshua had never tried to hide his actions from Hayden. Though a brilliant businessman, as a loyal husband, he sucked. Not that Audrey Sutherland seemed too bothered by his cheating. How could she when she stayed? Whenever Hayden delivered an excuse about her husband's whereabouts, his wife always paused and stated her pat answer.

*When my husband is* finished, *please have him call his* wife.

Oh yeah, she knew. Hayden had known Audrey for nineteen years—well, as much as the housekeeper's daughter could know the regal lady of the manor—and the reigning Houston socialite was not a stupid woman. So either she didn't care, or she craved this lifestyle and the governor's mansion too much to allow her husband's side slap-and-tickle to make her leave Joshua's side.

What must it have been like for Griffin growing up, knowing his parents weren't faithful to each other? Having a ringside seat to infidelity and the mockery of marriage?

He'd never spoken so candidly of his father's adultery before—he hadn't mentioned it at all—but since she doubted Joshua's serial cheating had begun when she'd started working for him, Griffin had to have known.

Was that why he couldn't commit? Why he'd walked away from her so easily?

Shaking her head, she squelched the spurt of sympathy. He might not have had a great example of matrimony and fidelity with his parents, but his grandparents had been together for decades. Happily. So no. He didn't get that pass.

"Why would Joshua blackmail you to return home?" Evade. That was her strategy rather than admit he might have a point. "Why wouldn't he just ask you?"

"Because the answer would've been no." Again, flint entered his eyes. He set his cup on the counter. "He needs me here to complete his picture of the perfect, loving, non-dysfunctional family so he can dupe the Texan public into voting for him for governor."

Unease flickered inside her chest. That seemed so...wrong. Blackmailing his son? Even if Joshua figured Griffin would say no if he'd asked, forcing him to comply by undermining him? The tactic was...extreme. And distasteful. Still...

"I can't believe you didn't tell him to go to hell. Why did you cave? I'm sure there're other pieces of property out there."

His lips twisted into a cruel caricature of a smile, his gaze hooded. "I have my reasons."

None of which he would be sharing with her, apparently. The knowledge shouldn't have stung, but it did.

Shoving off the counter, he rounded the bar and strode past her. "Instead of going into the office you'll be coming here every day. My cousin Ryder is letting me use his place as a home base for the next couple of weeks while he's out of the country. I have the back room set up as a temporary office."

"So we'll actually be working?" she drawled.

He flicked her a glance. "I do run a business. Just because I'm side-lined here doesn't mean I'm going to abandon it."

Shame sidled across her conscience. Regardless of how he'd left Texas, he hadn't sat idle for the past few years. She'd read the report on him and his construction company before passing it on to Joshua. Griffin, though considered an upstart by some, was nonetheless well respected as an honest, demanding but fair businessman who prided himself on quality work.

He'd accomplished what he'd set out to do. Become his own man and earn his success on his merit without the connections—and weight—of the Sutherland name.

"Before we get started, your father asked me to give this to you." She removed a black, leather folder from her bag and extended it toward him.

Accepting the portfolio as if it were a hissing snake, he flipped it open, perused it. His eyebrows crashed down into a dark, forbidding vee. "You have to be fucking kidding me," he muttered.

"Bad news, I take it," she observed. "What? Did he demand you get a haircut?" He still sported the man bun, though this morning, more blond strands escaped the tie at the back of his head, lending him a just-scraped-it-back-after-a-hot-night-of-sex look. With the long hair and beard shading his jaw and encircling his mouth, he should've appeared unkempt. Instead, he carried off the sexy lumbersexual look that seemed all the rage on man candy Pinterest boards with an authenticity that was natural and just hot as hell.

Griffin shifted his attention from the folder to her. She prayed that incisive, penetrating stare couldn't read her thoughts.

"Apparently, my presence is requested at a gala tonight. Formal dress required." He sneered. "I hope Joshua is paying you overtime,

Hayden."
    Well damn.

# CHAPTER SIX

Hell.

This was his idea of hell.

Griffin white-knuckled the glass of Scotch in his hand—no frou-frou champagne for him. If he was going to survive this night, he needed something stronger than bubbly wine. And from the size of this crowd, this drink wasn't going to be his last.

Smothering a sigh, he sipped from the tumbler, savoring the smoky flavor and smoothness of the liquor. One good thing he could say about the rarefied Houston social elite. They didn't scrimp on the good alcohol.

He scanned the crowded ballroom packed with bejeweled and gowned women and tuxedoed men, and gritted his teeth. He hadn't missed this whole dog-and-pony show while he'd been gone. Of course he'd attended business dinners and events when whining and dining clients had been required. And if he'd wanted to seek out this particular scene, Miami sat just two hours north from where he lived. The name Sutherland would have assuredly paved his way into those exclusive circles. But he'd purposefully avoided it, avoided...this.

People whose main concern wasn't the cause they'd gathered to "shed a light on." What was it tonight? Animal cruelty? Literacy? Save the apple blossom? He snorted, downing another drink of Scotch. He doubted most of them knew. They were here to see and be seen. To forge business and social connections. Feed on the carrion of gossip.

All the while wearing tens of thousands of dollars in clothes and jewelry that could've been donated to the charity they celebrated.

Useless. Aimless.

And maybe he was just a bitter, cynical son-of-a-bitch.

"I still don't understand why you insisted I attend tonight."

Griffin found his first smile of the night as the low, irritated grumble reached his ears. Hayden. The only thing making this evening bearable.

"I already told you," he said. "All for one, and one for all."

She snorted. "Last time I checked, I hadn't volunteered to be a damn Musketeer. I think you mean this is another example of misery loving company."

He didn't reply. Because then he would have to confess that he'd lied to her earlier about why he'd demanded Joshua assign her to him for his time in Houston. Making her suffer had sounded better than he didn't feel quite so alone with her. That her presence calmed the prowling, restless beast inside him. It always had, and even now, when he couldn't trust her with the real reason behind his decision to accept his father's terms—as long as she worked for Joshua, he couldn't entrust the truth about Sarah with Hayden—her effect on him remained unchanged. Not to mention that he just fucking loved looking at her.

Like tonight.

Though he preferred the curls, her sleek, straightened hair streamed down her back like a dark brown waterfall of the purest silk. His fingers itched to caress it...tug it. Fucking mess it up. In deference to the occasion, she'd donned a floor-length gown, the deep emerald not too flashy. She'd probably worn it, hoping to blend in and not draw attention to herself.

If that had been her intention, he could've told her she wasted her time. Hayden could wear a potato sack and still garner notice. A man would carefully study the curve of her breasts, breathlessly waiting to see if the full, gorgeous flesh would press against the material. Scrutinize the sway of her hips for just a glimpse of the feminine flare that elicited dirty, raw fantasies. Fantasies of gripping those hips while thrusting into her tight, fluttering pussy, his stomach slapping the perfect globes of her ass.

The dress she wore tonight hid nothing of her sensual, Venus-inspired body. From the front, it appeared modest, the neckline high, the skirt full. But then when she turned around. Fuck. The rich material disappeared, exposing an alluring expanse of dusky, toffee-colored skin from the base of her neck to the shallow dip under her spine. Saint and sinner. Innocent and vixen. Ingénue and siren.

Was Griffin the only man here who could claim intimate knowledge of which accurately described her?

*He doesn't know how hard and messy you like it, does he, baby? He doesn't know how you love your pussy eaten then fucked? How you love a dick thrusting between those gorgeous tits. He doesn't know how much you scream when a cock is sliding into your sweet, tight ass.*

The taunt he'd uttered to her in Florida haunted him now. Tormented him. No, he hadn't been chaste these past years. And it was incredibly chauvinistic to expect Hayden to have been. But damn if the thought of any man knowing what her cries and pleas as she orgasmed sounded like didn't send him down the crimson-paved road of rage. He gripped the glass tighter, the fingers of his free hand curling into a fist. Griffin had been responsible for teaching her the pleasures of sex, of introducing her to the headiness of causing one's lover's body to shake and tremble in ecstasy. Then he'd walked away. Now he damned anyone who'd taken his place.

He stared down into the amber liquor. Yeah, he was definitely going to need more of these if he was going to survive not just the minutiae of the evening but these murderous urges as well.

"You look beautiful tonight," he murmured.

Her head jerked up, her gorgeous hazel eyes widening. Her lush lips, slicked in a vibrant red, parted, and he heard the soft gasp that escaped. Her gaze dipped to his mouth, lingering, before lifting once more. Secrets. So many secrets swam in the gold and green depths. Secrets to which he was no longer privy. Ones he wasn't even sure he wanted to know.

"Thank you," she whispered. "You clean up well yourself, Samson."

He smiled at her reference to his hair, resisting the need to rub a palm over his newly tamed beard. Shaving himself clean had been out of the question. Not out of rebellion, but because this—hair length and beard—was him. Still, he'd shaped the hair around his jaw and mouth for the occasion. Had brushed his shoulder length hair into a knot at the back of head. Then he'd donned a dark blue, pinstriped three-piece suit. Fuck the tuxedo.

"And thank you for coming."

Instead of pointing out that she hadn't had a choice in the manner, she dipped her chin in acknowledgment, a small smile ghosting over her mouth. "You're welcome."

"Griffin."

Many people called him by his name, but only one woman stated it in that smooth, melodic tone that declared the very best breeding.

Glancing up, he turned and faced Audrey Sutherland.

"Hello, Mother." Leaning forward, he brushed his lips over her cheek. Her light, floral scent—the same one she'd worn since he was a kid—greeted him. The familiarity tugged at his heart. For all her You-are-a-Sutherland-first-and-foremost bullshit, he loved and had missed her. Unlike Joshua, she hadn't been hard or punishing. Just absent. "Gorgeous as always. You wear thirty well."

Pleasure lit the blue eyes she'd passed down to him as she shook her head. "You always had too much charm for your own good."

"Ah, charm." He cocked his head to the side. "I believe our Irish ancestors called it blarney. Or bullshit."

"Griffin, please." She tapped his arm, but her frown was compromised by the humor glinting in her gaze. Then she sighed. "Son, your hair. I swear, you still look like one of those lumberjacks. I was hoping you'd cut it since my party. No wonder you haven't come to see me before now."

"It's called lumbersexual, I believe. And I did come by the house, but you were at a Save the Petunias meeting, or something like that, so you missed me."

She shook her head. "Incorrigible," she said. "Your sister is here with Cash. So are your father and brother."

The warmth that had eddied in his chest cooled a bit. Not at the thought of seeing his baby sister and her new fiancé. Griffin had met Cash, and he was a good man. Good for Callie. Especially after the cheating asshole she'd married and divorced. His little sister had grown in the time Griffin had last seen her, grabbing ahold of the life she wanted even if it flouted what their parents believed she should want. It was the mention of Joshua and Josh that had him gritting his teeth and scoping out the nearest exit. Like elements with opposing, combustible components, the three of them couldn't remain in the same area for long periods of time before blowing the fuck up.

"Hayden." Frost infiltrated his mother's voice, the bite of it taking him aback. From one moment to the next Audrey transformed from exasperated, indulgent mother into haughty society matron. "What are you doing here?"

"I invited her," Griffin said before Hayden could reply. "I've borrowed her from Joshua for the next two weeks since I still have to work while I'm at his beck and call."

"Griffin, really. Why you insist on being so disrespectful toward your father..." At his arched eyebrow, she didn't continue but her pursed lips relayed her displeasure. "Still, bringing," a pause, "*your assistant* to a social event isn't appropriate. She belongs in the office, not the ballroom."

Beside him, Hayden stiffened. He didn't glance down, knowing if he glimpsed a hint of hurt on her features, he would say something that might cause his mother embarrassment and pain. More importantly, he didn't want to draw even more of Audrey's apparent but confusing disdain toward Hayden. Griffin would leave once more in a couple of weeks; she had to remain behind, working for his father and still dealing with his mother.

"Careful, Mother," he drawled, not bothering to blunt the edge to his words. "Your claws are showing." Trusting himself to peer down at Hayden, he gently squeezed her waist, ignoring the further tensing of her curvaceous frame. "Hayden, would you mind hunting down Edward Grey for me? I wanted to speak with him earlier."

To her credit, she didn't bat an eye at the blatant lie. She just nodded, murmured a soft "excuse me" and several moments later, disappeared in the crowd.

"You want to explain to me what that was about, Mother?" he growled. "You've known Hayden since she was seven years old, yet you treated her like the help right now. It was uncalled for and mean-spirited." He longed to add, her mother was also the only maid who hasn't fucked your husband. But that, too, would've been mean-spirited.

She ignored his demand for an explanation, instead waving at an older couple and a younger woman who neared them. "Henry and Michelle, please come meet my long-lost son." Her perfect hostess smile firmly fixed into place, she placed a hand on Griffin's arm. "Griffin, these are my dear friends Henry and Michelle Granger, and their daughter Candace. Henry, Michelle, Candace, this is my youngest son, Griffin Sutherland."

"Dear friends" was relative for his mother. That could mean she'd known the handsome couple and their lovely daughter for five years or five minutes. In their world, everyone was a "dear friend"—even when you wouldn't piss on them if they were on fire.

"Nice to meet you." Henry pumped his hand, both his and his wife's gazes avidly curious. They probably couldn't wait to go share that they'd met the infamous Sutherland black sheep.

"Honey, you and Candace are both University of Texas alumni. She just graduated last year." Audrey beamed fondly at the younger woman.

And Griffin barely restrained his eye roll. The police had a name for his mother's actions. Entrapment.

"Congratulations," he said, nodding at Candace. "What was your major?"

"Business management," Henry bragged, replying before his daughter could.

"You two already have something in common," Audrey pointed out. "Why don't you become better acquainted? Henry, Michelle? There are some friends I would like to introduce you to." With that, his mother departed, the older Grangers following in her wake like she was the Pied Piper.

"Subtle as a Mack truck, isn't she?" he drawled.

Candace smiled, her green eyes alight with laughter. "I have the tire tracks on my back to prove it."

He chuckled, surprised by the woman's dry wit. Candace Granger was a classic Texas Rose—perfectly coiffed blonde hair, porcelain skin, lovely emerald eyes and a slender body encased in a dress that was probably straight off a Parisian runway. He understood why his mother had decided to play matchmaker. Yet, as undeniable as her beauty was, he appreciated it like a beautiful painting or a stunning sunset. Admired it but didn't want to own it. Claim it.

Because she didn't have wild, chocolate curls or hazel, almond-shaped eyes that a man could willingly drown in. She didn't possess a mouth that called to mind all things sinful or skin that was caramel dusted with vanilla. She didn't boast a body full of sexy curves and dips.

She wasn't Hayden.

Fuck. When would he stop comparing other women to her? He might have left her all those years ago, but *she'd* never left *him*.

Resisting the urge to search her out among the guests, he forced another smile for Candace. "Since I'm sure there are at least three pairs of eyes focused on us at the moment, can I escort you to your table?"

"Far be it for me to disappoint them," she said, slipping her hand into the crook of his proffered arm. "I'd hate for them to think all their hard work was wasted."

He caught the flirtatious invitation as well as the interest in her gaze. Any other time, he would've jumped on both. But becoming involved with a woman who was the daughter of his parents' friends? Why not go grab a noose and loop it around his own neck? He was here for two weeks, and starting a relationship wasn't on the carefully planned agenda his father had set out. Although, Joshua would probably amend the itinerary if he thought Griffin hooking up with Candace was advantageous to him.

Still his life was in Florida. And after he served his time in Houston, he would return there, with the deed to the property that should've been his in the first place. And somehow he couldn't picture Candace Granger living in Blackpool, Florida.

*But Hayden…*

Quickly, he shook the insidious thought free. She'd made it abundantly clear where her loyalties lay. Here. With his father here in Houston. And if the thought gripped his stomach in a vicious twist, well…tough shit.

***

The two made a striking couple.

Hayden studied Griffin and the tall, model-thin, gorgeous blonde standing beside him. The one Audrey hadn't wasted anytime introducing him to as soon as she'd sent Hayden on her way—away from her son. To be fair, it'd been Griffin who'd asked her to run the fictitious errand, but Hayden had leaped at the chance to escape his mother's condescending, haughty gaze. And though, Hayden had sat beside Griffin at the table, she'd maintained the distance even through dinner. Because in that instant, Hayden had gone from multi-degreed, professional businesswoman to "the help", and she hated herself for allowing Audrey to make her feel small, not good enough.

*"It's not what they call you but what you answer to."* Her mother's advice drifted across her mind. True, but the problem was sometimes a

47

person answered out of habit.

When Hayden had finally risen from the abyss of grief she'd tumbled head-first into after Griffin walked out, she'd refused to let anyone make her feel unworthy again. Never permit the greasy oil of shame to slide through her belly or permeate her skin. But all it'd required for that five year resolution to quiver and threaten to shatter was Griffin reentering her life.

Stoic, Hayden made herself stare at Griffin and the woman who'd found him and attached herself to his side as soon as dinner ended. She was golden. Perfect. This was the partner his parents wanted for him. Not the second generation Latino daughter of their housekeeper. At one time, she'd fooled herself into believing love could conquer all. That her and Griffin's disparaging backgrounds and lifestyles didn't matter—not when they loved each other. That naïve, glass-slippers-dancing-in-her-head girl had died a painful, disillusioned death. The woman born in her place knew better. Love was an excuse, and at times a weapon. People used it to rationalize their behavior and wielded it like a broadsword to maim and cut down.

Most of all though?

Love was a crock of shit.

"Hello, Hayden."

She turned and met a dark gaze identical to her employer's. Probably because Joshua had bequeathed it to him.

"Hello, Josh," she said, surprise winging through her. Griffin's older brother by two years—and the eldest sibling—was a replica of their father. Black hair, dark brown-almost-black eyes, handsome. While she and Griffin had shared a close relationship, hers with Josh had been distant, polite. And that hadn't changed in the years since childhood. Other than courteous greetings at the office when their paths crossed, they weren't friends. So him voluntarily seeking her out had her what-the-hell radar dinging.

"You look beautiful tonight."

She blinked. *O-kay*. "Thank you," she said slowly. "I don't mean to be rude, Josh, but is there something I can do for you?"

A corner of his mouth quirked up in a half-smile. The man truly was good-looking. If she peeped over his shoulder, she would probably catch at least a dozen women eyeing him. Sexy, successful, and a Sutherland heir. A prize catch. So what the hell was he doing talking to her instead of charming the panties off of those women?

"I missed you around the office today. Dad said you were helping Griffin out while he was in town."

"Yes." She forced herself not to glance in Griffin and his new…friend's direction. "For the next couple of weeks I'm his assistant instead of your father's."

"How's it working out?"

She hiked up a shoulder. "It's only been one day and no blood has been shed so I'd say we're off to a fabulous start."

Josh chuckled. "That sounds about right with Griffin." His laughter eased into a smile, but the intensity in his dark stare belied the softness flirting with his mouth. "You two always were close, though. If I remember correctly, you were the only one who could handle him. So I think he's in the right hands."

Unease flickered inside her chest. "I don't think 'handle' is accurate. No one can handle Griffin." Even Joshua had found out forcing Griffin to do anything he didn't want to do was like trying to saddle a gust of wind. Unwise and dangerous.

Josh cocked his head to the side, his regard still unwavering, incisive. "And I believe you underestimate yourself, Hayden," he murmured.

The unease breathed and expanded into an agitation that crawled under her skin. *He couldn't know…could he…?* It was possible if…

"If you'll excuse me." She didn't wait for his reply but skirted around him and headed toward the exit. Dinner was over, and she was officially off the clock. Griffin had made her attend the gala so they could both suffer. Well, he didn't appear tormented. And she'd served enough time tonight; she was granting herself probation.

Fresh, warm night air hit her face and bared arms. The inside of the ballroom hadn't seemed cloying until she tilted her head back and inhaled a deep, perfume-and-cologne free breath. Tension eked from her body, and a weight shifted off her chest. Freedom from pretentious conversation, false laughter, fake people and the glittery trappings. Was this really what she worked her ass off to have? To be a part of? If she were accepted by them, would that make her feel whole?

"Where are you going?"

A shiver danced down her spine. She closed her eyes. So much for early probation. "I didn't think you would mind if I called it a night."

Not when he held court with Ms. Texas on his arm. God, she needed to go home. The snarkiness was getting out of hand. Maybe after a hot shower and a good night's sleep, the tight band that had been constricting her chest since she'd first spied him with the other woman would ease. Maybe after some time and distance she could convince herself that she didn't give a damn.

But with the image of him and the blonde fresh in her mind, with his dark and delicious scent tickling her nose, neither was possible.

"Well, I do mind. You came with me, you'll leave with me."

"I'm sure your mother and new friend would have something to say about that." Damn. If she could kick her own ass, her size seven would be firmly planted back there. Heat streamed up her neck and poured into her face. She'd sounded like a shrew. Worse. A jealous shrew. "Never mind. Forget I—"

"What? Forget you said it?" One moment, the night air caressed her back and shoulders, and in the next, hot, hard muscle pressed against her. Jesus, he must have a furnace burning beneath his skin. Or maybe that was the flames of arousal inside her. Licking at her, searing her. "Answer me, Hayden," he growled. "Do you want me to forget?"

A tremulous puff of air escaped her lips. Not *that* voice. The one that had instructed her, commanded her to touch him, suck him...fuck him. That voice had happily led her skipping down a path of sin. "Yes," she whispered.

"Why?" He tucked a strand of hair behind her ear, his long, blunt-tipped fingers teasing the outer shell.

She locked her teeth against the groan that crawled up her throat, but couldn't do a damn thing about the tremble in her thighs. Or the beading of her nipples. Or the empty, *hungry* clenching in her pussy. The power of her need—need elicited by one rather innocuous touch—sent desperation surging through her, combating the desire. This fucking unwanted, resented desire.

"Why, baby?" He grasped her shoulders, turned her around to face him. Cradling her face in his big palm, he pressed his thumb to her bottom lip. Her teeth scraped the tender skin inside her mouth, and she moaned at the slight edge of pain his firm, dominant touch elicited. It echoed inside of her, its call expanding and rebounding until need resonated through every organ, every limb like an erotic sonar. "You want me to make you answer my question?" he purred.

*Yes. Make me.*

She didn't voice the plea, but maybe her whimper provided enough of a response. Because his mouth slammed down over hers, conquering, taking, fucking. Not gentle. Not coaxing or questioning. The five years that had separated them might as well as not have existed. There was no hesitation, no relearning. His tongue thrust past her parted lips, sweeping in and tangling with hers, demanding she duel with him, giving her what she loved as if their last kiss had been seconds ago instead of years. He feasted on her, one hand abandoning her cheek to slide to the nape of her neck and the other stroking down her spine to her ass, cupping her flesh, holding her steady for the carnal devastation that was his kiss.

A low, keening cry rose from her throat. The taste of him flooded into her, and moisture pricked her closed eyes at her first savoring in so long. *God, so long.* His rain and wind flavor seemed sharper, more intense. And she lapped it up. Fisting the lapels of his jacket, she rose on her tiptoes, silently begging for more. Begging to be branded. Begging to be taken. She angled her head, opened wider for him, surrendering, submitting. Her nipples tightened, pressing against her dress as her pussy swelled, clenched, moistened. Preparing itself for the deeper invasion that his mouth mimicked and promised…

*Shit, what was she doing?*

Gasping, she wrenched her head back. And when he followed, intent on recapturing her mouth, she jerked out of his hold, stumbling before righting herself.

For several long moments, they stared at each other, their harsh breathing the only sound in the silent night air. Lust tautened his features, stretching his skin over his patrician facial bones. His eyes glittered blue fire, lips were damp and swollen. She remembered this expression well. It haunted her in the darkest hours of the night, tempting and tormenting her with what she had and lost.

Glancing away, she exhaled and retreated another step.

"I want you to forget because I don't care," she rasped. Lied. "You should return inside. Your father and mother will be wondering where you are."

"You think I give a fuck about what they want?" he demanded, voice rough with the hungry desire that still lit his eyes like a flame. He shifted forward, eliminating the space she'd placed between them. "Hayden, goddamnit—" Hard fingers closed around her upper arm, not bruising, but again, she yanked out of his hold as if he singed her skin.

"Do you know why your mother can't stand the sight of me?" she blurted out. "She knows, Griffin. She knows about us." He froze, and she took immediate advantage, edging back, out of his reach. She laughed, and the chuckle scraped her throat. "You were right earlier. I regularly lie to her about her husband's whereabouts, but that isn't why she's so cold to me. I dared to become involved with her son. She tolerated our friendship when we were kids, but sleeping with you? Thinking I could be part of your family, your circle? Then driving you away? That was unforgivable."

"That's ridiculous," he snapped. "You had nothing to do with why I left."

"And could do nothing to make you stay," she said, for a moment, the pain as fresh, as wrenching as it'd been that night. "Doesn't matter, though. It's what she believes. She told me."

His sensual lips flattened into a grim line. "Tell me."

"One afternoon, she came to the office, and your father wasn't in. I tried to talk to her, because while she'd always been distant, she'd never been dismissive or unkind. That's when she let me know how she'd come by your apartment one evening and saw me leaving. Saw you kiss me. About two months later, you left home. She blamed me. You were content before me. So it was my fault her son left and didn't return for years. Because I had the audacity to reach for what wasn't mine."

"That's bullshit." He advanced a step forward. "We both know it's bullshit."

"Is it?" she whispered.

"What the fuck are you talking about, Hayden? You aren't why—"

"You left. I know. She has that all wrong. But the rest of it? For a time, I did believe you were mine. That I could be a part of your family instead of serving it. That what we had surpassed status, money, our circumstances. I loved you, and thought it was enough. That *I* was enough."

Shadows crept into his eyes, darkening them. His lashes lowered. "Baby..."

"No," she cut off whatever he would've said. Whatever platitude or apology that would shred her and leave the ribbons littering the sidewalk. "I'm only telling you this because none of it matters anymore. It's in the past. Here—right now—is what's important. While you might not give a fuck what your parents want, I have to. I work for him, and have to deal with her. In two weeks, you're back in Florida, but I won't be. I live here. My life is here. And I can't..." *Let you back in.* "Let you make it more difficult when you won't be here for the fall out. So please." She waved toward the building's entrance. "Go back in there. Hold up your end of the bargain you have with Joshua so you can get your property and put Houston behind you."

*Put me behind you.*

Again.

He'd nearly destroyed her when he'd left the last time. And in two weeks, he would walk out once more. Whatever the cost, she couldn't allow herself to be wreckage he left in his wake.

# CHAPTER SEVEN

Griffin raised his hand to knock on the door, but at the last second hesitated before rapping his knuckles against the wood. An unfamiliar case of nerves attacked him, rattling inside his gut.

"Fuck," he muttered, dragging his hand over his hair. Dumb as hell, standing outside a woman's apartment like a damn stalker. Still… He couldn't bring himself to knock.

Goddamn. At some point between the gala four nights ago—and that kiss that had him within seconds of coming in his pants—and tonight, he'd lost his nerve and his dick. He and Hayden had been walking on egg shells around each other, being polite, avoiding mention of anything personal. Griffin hadn't insisted she join him on any additional parties and dinners his father planned, and she didn't offer to attend. Didn't mean he didn't miss her like an amputated limb.

Pinching the bridge of his nose, he squeezed his eyes shut. God, he couldn't wipe the image of her face—her hazel eyes bright with passion then dull with sadness, her lovely features tight with pain—from his mind. He'd been the cause of all the emotion. While he loved that he'd had her whimpering into his mouth, desperate for his touch, for what he could give her, he bled inside at the hurt, the disillusionment. Since she'd come back into his life, Hayden had worn this tough outer shell that would've made a turtle envious. But for an instant, she'd allowed him a glimpse into the woman behind the barrier, and he'd seen the pain he'd inflicted, the damage he'd wreaked.

He, who had detested the hurt and neglect his parents so carelessly meted out with their selfishness and vanity, had done the very same thing to the person who'd mattered most in his life. To hell with a bitter pill. The knowledge was like swallowing a cyanide capsule.

Maybe he could've taken Hayden with him… *No.* He shook his head. Insisting she remain and finish college had been one of his most selfless acts in his life. It would've been so easy to say, yes, pack up and come with me. But it would've robbed her, too. Of her education, her future. Of her opportunities. Of *her*.

Clenching his jaw, he knocked on her apartment door.

Seconds that felt like eons passed, but just as he lifted his fist to rap on the weathered wood again, the metallic sound of a lock twisting reached him. The door swung open, and whatever he'd been about to say withered and died on his tongue.

*Goddamn.*

He'd seen Hayden in skinny jeans, business attire and a ball gown. As gorgeous as she was in all of them, this woman in a white, men's tank and tiny, pink sleep shorts beat them all. Her beautiful, heavy breasts pushed against the top, and through the thin material, black lace taunted him like a red flag waved before a raging bull. The shorts skimmed over the sensual flare of her hips, stopping mere inches below the pussy he hungered for with a desperate need that should've scared him. Would've scared him if he could think. Long, slim legs seemed to stretch for miles, ending in dainty feet, toes painted a vibrant, surprising neon green. The incongruous color almost made him smile. Almost. It was hard to show amusement when his zipper was creating a stencil against his dick.

He dragged his gaze back up her petite figure, lingering over her breasts once more, remembering the feel of the hard tips on his tongue, recalling the husky moans she emitted when he tugged and sucked on her beaded flesh. How her sex would squeeze his cock when he tongued her nipples while he was deep inside her. How she begged him to eat her pussy while he pinched those nipples. God, she used to love the hell out of that.

Fingers curling into fists, he raised his scrutiny higher, finally meeting the hazel eyes that shamed every woman he'd ever met into the realm of ordinary.

"I'm going to fuck you." The declaration, raw and stark in the silence, abraded his throat as it escaped. He hadn't meant to utter it—hadn't come over here for that—but he refused to rescind his intention. Not when it was the truth. Not when lust poured through him so thick and hot, it seemed to weigh him down. Not when he could barely breathe past the need.

Her eyes widened a fraction, but when he stepped over the threshold and quietly shut the door behind him, she didn't utter a word. Didn't retreat from him. And that silent acquiescence snapped the frayed leash on his control.

A veil of crimson slammed down over his vision as he leaped on her. He crashed his mouth to hers, wheeling around and back-pedaling her toward the nearest wall. Burrowing his fingers in her unruly curls, he thrust his tongue between her lips, claiming all the sweetness inside. For himself. His alone. Swirling, licking, sucking... The kiss was messy, wild, untampered. No skill, just need. The need for more. Always the need for more. He wanted her to willingly give him everything. Her mouth. Her touch. Her screams. Her pussy. Her trust. Her heart...

Ripping his mouth away, he shook his head as if he could unsettle that last thought. She'd given her heart to him once, and he didn't have the right to ask it of her again. But this...sex, fucking. It'd always been good—goddamn apocalyptic—between them. She would give him her body, her pleasure, her orgasms. It would have to be enough. For both of them.

She clamped his head between her hands, her short fingernails scraping his scalp. He groaned, obeying her silent plea and taking her mouth again. For just a moment, he allowed her to commandeer the lead, let her do the taking. Fuck, her need was intoxicating, like the strongest, most potent liquor in his veins. Little whimpers escaped her, greedy sounds like flicks of her tongue over his cock. Cupping the back of her thigh, he hiked her leg up, held it wide. And ground his throbbing, hard dick against the pad of her pussy. God, she was soft. Even through his jeans and the flimsy material of her shorts, he swore he could feel her heat. Circling his hips, he repeated the movement, dragging his erection up her slit, rolling over her clit.

She cried out, the back of her head hitting the wall with a muted thump. Her soft pants echoed in the room, and they weren't enough. He wanted—needed—her screams. Releasing her leg, he jerked her tank top up, leaving the material bundled above the lace-covered flesh he bared. Still not enough. He yanked the cups down, the cups holding her breasts up as if serving them to him like a delicious treat he'd long been denied.

Passion made him rough, and when he latched onto a dark nipple, he wasn't gentle. From the dark, heavy moan she released, Hayden didn't seem to mind. Didn't mind the hard drawing or rapid flicks. Or the pinches and tweaks of his fingers on its twin. Lifting his head, he studied the damp flesh, the flush painting her chest. Unable to resist, he dipped for another taste, coiling his tongue around a tip, tugging on the rigid peak. Growling, he cupped both breasts, pushing them high and together until her nipples almost grazed one another. Fuck, the sight of her. Lowering his mouth to her, he sucked both tips, stroking them with his tongue, scraping them with his teeth. Loving every cry and sob he elicited from her.

She writhed against him, her body trapped between the wall, his body and his mouth. Her fingers twisted in his hair, yanked on the strands, holding him to her. Encircling her wrists, he forced her hands from him, cuffed them to the wall on either side of her hips. She whined a protest, but he didn't heed it, instead licking a sensual path down her torso, over her soft belly until his lips bumped the band of her shorts. He tightened his clasp on her wrists, silently ordering her to stay put before yanking the bottoms and her panties down her hips and long legs until the material pooled at her feet.

*Fuck.*

The prettiest pussy he'd ever seen.

For a second, he closed his eyes, but immediately reopened them, loathe to miss a single moment of the gorgeous woman in front of him. Totally bare of hair, the caramel and honey folds glistened with evidence of her desire. This was new. Not the cream slicking her lips—no, he'd witnessed that often on her, how wet she could get for him. The shaved pussy. When had she started that? And for whom… A shaft of jealousy pierced him, for an instant dislodging the clawing lust. His fingers tightened on her thighs, part of him longing to command the answers from her. But the other side—the animalistic, primal side—wanted to mark her, stake his ownership on this woman, on this pussy by reminding her who it belonged to.

Wedging his shoulder under her thigh, he spread her open for him and dove into her. Again, tenderness hovered far beyond his reach.

Too much time had passed. Too much hunger had built up for gentleness. Not when her musky, sweet, thick scent filled his nostrils. Not when for the first time in years her folds parted under the stroke of his tongue and her juice slid across his taste buds. Her sharp, tormented cries caressed his ears. He lapped at her clit, flicking it before returning to the core of her and fucking her with his mouth. More moisture seeped from her, and he feasted on it, claiming each drop as his due.

Nails pricked his scalp, scraped his shoulders and neck. She bucked and rolled as if unsure whether she wanted to escape him or urge him on. Ripping the decision from her, he clamped firm fingers around her hip, holding her while he plunged two fingers inside her pussy. The slick, strong walls of her sex immediately clutched and squeezed him. So fucking tight. Like a hot little fist. His dick jumped in his pants, begging for that same erotic embrace. Coiling his tongue around her clit, he drew on the engorged nub, knowing from experience she loved a firm suck. Knew alternating with long, sweeps over the sensitive bundle of nerves would shove her to orgasm.

Twisting his wrist, he corkscrewed his fingers high into her pussy, treating her to grinding thrust after thrust, his knuckles smacking her swollen lips. The muscles quivered and spasmed around him, her clit pulsing under his caresses.

Her thighs clenched, her body stiffened, but instead of delivering the last plunge and stroke that would send her tumbling over the edge, he withdrew, surging to his feet. He ripped at the closure to his pants, wrenched down the zipper and thrust a hand inside to fist his cock. Hissing at the pleasure and ache, he freed his dick, squeezing the base hard, afraid just the draft of cool air over the swollen, damp tip could make him blow.

A soft gasp had his head lifting. Hayden stared down at him, her hazel eyes bright, slashes of pink tingeing her cheekbones. The tip of her tongue swept over her lush bottom lip, wetting the curve, inviting him to repeat the action. He dropped his attention back down to his cock, wondering how she saw him. Intimidating? He could understand that. With the ruddy, bulbous head shiny with pre-cum, and veins lacing the heavy, thick stalk, he appeared almost brutish in his need. But that wasn't fear that glittered in her gaze. Maybe a little apprehension, but definitely excitement. Passion. Hunger.

She wanted him. Wanted him inside her, stretching her, burning her, filling her. And damn it, he craved the same.

Stroking his fist up his erection, he grimaced, bracing himself against the lash of pleasure. Hold on. He had to hold on until her pussy was wrapped tight around him, her silken, muscular hold gripping him, milking him. Then he could let go.

"Are you still on the Pill?" They were the first words he'd spoken since his announcement at her front door, and his voice seemed to boom in the charged silence. Lust sharpened the question, roughened it. She jerked her attention from his dick to his face, eyes wide. "Hayden," he growled.

A short nod of her head.

"I'm clean, baby. I don't fuck without a condom. But you..." A shudder rippled through him as he stroked himself once more. "I don't want anything between us."

A long pause where he held his breath, and when she again gave him a nod, he exhaled, relief pouring through him in a deluge. Until that second when she agreed, he hadn't admitted to himself how important her answer was to him. Even if she didn't realize what her submission meant, he understood this woman had to trust him to some degree to permit him inside her with no barrier.

Thank fuck. He couldn't stand even the thin, latex layer separating him from her.

"Put your arms around me," he murmured, moving in between her legs. Not waiting for her obedience, he hiked her up, wrapping her legs around his hips. His cockhead notched against her grasping entrance, but instead of immediately plunging into the smooth, two-sizes-too-small channel, he waited. Savoring this moment. Remembering in case he needed it to carry him through another five year absence.

"Griffin, please," she whispered, twisting as if trying to impale herself. He grunted against the glide of her wet heat over his flesh as well as her use of his given name. Not once since she'd walked back into his life had she uttered the shortened version of his name. With his cock kissing her pussy, he longed to hear it, have her murmur it, scream it...

Closing his eyes, he buried his face in the natural cradle between her shoulder and neck, and holding her steady in his arms, thrust deep in one stroke.

Or he tried.

Her flesh resisted him, clutching and seizing as if attempting to repel him rather than accept him. Still… He groaned, his hips instinctively flexing. Her sex gripped him, so hot, so wet, so fucking tight. If he had bruises covering his dick later, he wouldn't be surprised. Shifting her in his arms, he withdrew and slowly slid back in…and met the same resistance.

Plaintive whimpers penetrated the fog of lust enshrouding him. Hayden shuddered under him, her arms almost strangling him, her thighs quaking around his hips. Fuck, she wasn't a virgin. But damn if she wasn't as tight as one. As if she hadn't…

Oh fuck.

"Shh," he soothed, smoothing her wild tumble of curls away from her flushed, sweat-dampened face. Stroking the pained lines straining her face. "Easy, baby. Easy. Hayden," he called her name, firming his voice, placing a hard demand in the tone. When her lashes lifted, and her glazed eyes focused, he brushed a kiss across her trembling lips. "That's it, baby. Look at me. I wish you could feel what you're doing to my cock. To me. Squeezing me so tight with your perfect, pretty pussy. I could come right now, just fill you up with my cum. And God knows I want to. But I've waited too long, dreamed too much…" Again, he swept his mouth over hers. "I want to fuck you as long as possible. Feel you shake and moan around me. But I got to get in this pussy first, baby. You have to let me in."

Her breath quickened, the tautness easing from her features as desire softened them. Yeah, she'd always loved when he talked dirty to her. Already her flesh relaxed the slightest fraction, loosening its stranglehold on his dick.

"I want in, Hayden. I'll wait here all night until you do. It'll be worth it to fuck you, ride you. Explode inside you, feel you drown me in your sweet cream. I want all of that—I want to give it all to you. But you have to let me inside first, okay, baby?"

"Yes," she breathed, jerking her head up and down. "I want that. Want you."

"Fuck," he rasped, and covered her mouth in a deep, hard tangle of tongues and lips. "I love hearing you say that."

Slowly, he dragged his cock free of her grasping flesh, and just as deliberately eased back in, groaning as he gained another inch, her pussy granting him deeper access to the heart of her. Again, he repeated the action. And again. And again. Until both of them, covered in sweat, shook and quivered, and he was embedded fully in her sex.

"Goddamn, baby." He grunted, circled his hips, pressing his pelvis against her clit. "You're so goddamn sweet." Pulling free until only the head of his cock remained, he then plunged inside, the stroke smooth, meeting no struggle. Their moans punctuated the air like an erotic symphony. "Ready, Hayden?"

"Oh God, yes." Her fingers clutched his shoulders, and he shifted his hands to her ass, gripping her taut flesh, supporting her. Then he proceeded to fuck her like he promised. Hard. Rough. Without control, with abandon. Jesus Christ, her pussy sucked at him like a greedy mouth, swallowing him, engulfing him. It was just as he remembered... No. Better. Hotter. Dirtier. More.

The slap of skin against skin. The wet suction of her pussy releasing and accepting him. Her high, keening wails and screams and his dark groans. They filled the room, and he lost himself in them, in her. He pounded into her pussy without mercy, burying himself in her slick walls over and over again, unable to get enough. *Mine. Mine. Fucking mine.* The litany played in his head on a loop, and he clenched his teeth, afraid in this erotic storm he would utter the damning words.

Electric jolts sizzled in the base of his spine, tingled in his balls, signaling the onset of an orgasm that would make a mockery of every release he'd had in the past years. Needing her to be with him, he reached between them and circled his thumb over her clit, pressing and sweeping over the hard nub.

With one last scream, Hayden stiffened in his arms, her back bowing, her breasts quivering. Her pussy clamped down on his dick, seizing him, milking him. Slamming his fist against the wall, he thrust inside her once, twice, three times and exploded. Over and over he jetted cum, splashing her pussy, filling her. His head fell back on his shoulders, and he shook as the orgasm went on and on, emptying him of everything—his cum, his mind, his fucking soul.

# CHAPTER EIGHT

"When was the last time?"

Hayden stilled beside Griffin, her hand pausing mid-absent-caress over his chest. After that—what the hell should she call what happened against her apartment wall?—cataclysmic event with Griffin, they'd stumbled into her bedroom and fell to the bed. Only to repeat the event—because seriously it couldn't be called sex because regular sex just wasn't that good— again. This time slower, gentler, but just as hot. *God*, just as hot.

Not for the first time she asked herself what in God's name was she doing? Just four days ago she'd decided to keep as much distance as possible considering she had to work with him for the foreseeable future. She'd definitely resolved not to repeat the stupid mistake of kissing him. *Kissing him.* Not only had that resolution been an epic fail, but she'd fucked him. Let him back into her body without even a token fuss. Not even a half-hearted, *I don't think this is a good idea.* Nope, she'd just let him pin her against the wall and ride her like one of those horses his grandfather owned and bred.

Jesus, what had she been thinking?

But that was just it. She'd done so much thinking over the past few days—of the kiss, of his hands on her, of his delicious scent, of him with Texas Barbie—that it'd been like foreplay. So when he'd shown up at her door, gorgeous, brooding and almost seething with some emotion that fairly emanated from him, she'd been ready. And by ready, she meant wet. So fucking wet from just one look at his big,

ed in a white dress shirt and pants that probably cost
ardrobe, with that sexy bun of thick, golden hair and
d that framed his carnal, lush mouth.

'd been so…empty. Lonely. Not alive. And the
s she hadn't realized any of this until she'd heard
a Florida dive bar. He stirred something in her.
ll it a quickening; she called it lust.

y she'd surrendered so quickly. Even knowing
days he wouldn't be there. Because lust was
lize, easy to walk away from. And the heart
ecause it wouldn't be involved.

troked a palm up her spine, the calluses on his
shiver through her.

d her legs from his and sat up, dragging her
l, she didn't want to have this conversation.
.. Although, he'd probably guessed it. And
iliating?

ustled behind her and the mattress dipped.
rm fingers pinched her chin and turned her head.
Griffin's steady, piercing scrutiny as well as the grip on her face
refused to allow her to avoid him or the question.

"Three years," she blurted out, closing her eyes. His swift intake
of breath reached her ears, and as heat poured into her cheeks, she
jerked her head out of his grasp. She waited for the follow-up inquiry.
He wasn't a fool; he had to comprehend the implications behind the
long length of time. And he wouldn't be wrong.

But the questions didn't come. But his touch did. Feather light at
first. To the top of her spine, the nape of her neck, the skin across
her shoulders. Then in her hair, tangling, massaging her scalp until
she had to bite back a groan at the sensual and yet, comforting caress.
She pressed a cheek to her drawn up knees, locking her arms around
them.

"The year after you left I was like a zombie. Barely left my
apartment except for school. I didn't see anyone, didn't go anywhere,
didn't eat. I lost so much weight I thought Mama was going to start
force-feeding me." She huffed out a low chuckle, but with the weight
of that black time heavy on her, the soft laughter was void of humor.
"I was…lost. And for a while I didn't think I would get back to
myself, find who I'd been before…"

"I left," he murmured, his hand continuing its stroking.

She nodded. "Yes. After that year, I never wanted to be in that place again. Lose myself again. It was terrifying, and I needed my life back. I *needed* to be me again. To *feel* again." To discover who she was without him. "So I forced myself to start dating. There was one man who I liked. And trusted enough to," she paused, squeezing her legs, "have sex with."

His fingers stilled. And for a second tightened. Her scalp tingled from his grip on the curls, and she inhaled, attempting to stifle the lust that spiraled through her at the tiny pricks of pain. His breath deepened, roughened, and hers lowered to match his rhythm. A moment later, his hold eased but the need didn't.

"I went home and threw up. And again when I tried it a second time, thinking the first might've been a fluke. It hadn't been. I didn't bother after that. I couldn't—" She shrugged. Bear to have anyone's hands on me but yours.

"I'm fucking glad."

Surprise sucker punched the breath from her lungs. She jerked her head up, meeting his narrowed, heated stare.

"You're glad I've been lonely and unable have sex these past years?" she demanded, hating the slight tremble in her voice.

"Yes," he stated. "No matter how much of an asshole that makes me."

She curled her lip up in a sneer. "A hypocritical asshole considering you probably haven't led the life of a monk."

"No, I haven't."

Pain sliced her open, and she blinked against the agony of it. Stupid, so stupid to be hurt by his bald admission. She'd known as much. A man as sexual as him wouldn't go with—

She flew back on the mattress, her head hitting the pillow as a big, hard body covered hers. Griffin loomed above her, his palms planted on either side of her head. Several shorter strands of his hair swept forward, glancing over his sculpted cheekbones and rigid jaw. Emphasizing the blaze in his blue eyes.

"Damn it, Griffin," she snapped.

"You're right. I've fucked women." When she shoved against his shoulders, he clasped her wrists in one large hand and manacled them over her head. He gripped her chin with the other, forcing her to meet his gaze. "But I can only remember one thing about any of them. None were you."

Her heart—the traitorous, foolish organ—pounded in her chest. Hadn't it learned not to flutter and ache at pretty words? Didn't it remember the agony of having it ripped out of her chest by the man whose stare pierced hers, whose hips wedged in between her legs, whose cock pressed to her sex, setting her on fire? Lust, desire, passion—they were reactions, chemical responses. But love... Love was sacrifice, trust, commitment. Forever.

They didn't have that. At the end of his two weeks, Griffin would walk away from home, from her, again. She didn't fool herself into believing he would stay, that he could promise her forever and keep it. She didn't trust him not to hurt her. She didn't trust herself not to serve her heart up on a silver platter to be shattered again. Not with this man. When it came to Griffin, masochism seemed to be her default setting.

Lowering her lashes, she wiggled her hands until he set her free. Her wrists tingled from his implacable grip, and she stifled the urge to rub her skin in a vain effort to trap the sensation like a memento for when he left again.

"Why did you come by?" Yes, she was deflecting. And judging from the tightening of his lips, he recognized that tactic.

"Because the dinner party was missing something."

"What?"

"You."

Damn, he had to stop saying things like that. For her sanity, he had to stop.

She huffed out a dry, strained chuckle. "Right. Knowing your mother, she had several women lined up to keep you entertained and occupied. Including Miss Texas Barbie."

God, she needed to shut the hell up. Did she have a fucking off switch?

"Texas Barbie," he repeated. A corner of his mouth kicked up. "Are you referring to Candace?" She shrugged. Damn that, she wasn't saying one more word. Stupid shit seemed determined to fall off her tongue around him. "Yeah, she was there. Wait..." He cocked his head to the side. "Is she why you left the gala the other night?"

*Hell yes.* "No."

He studied her, and she fought not to struggle under its sharp, way-too-damn-incisive power.

"She's a beautiful woman," he murmured, his scrutiny roaming her face. "But she doesn't have unruly, chocolate curls that beg a man to tangle his fingers in them. She doesn't have chameleon hazel eyes that can change from brown to green to gold depending on her mood. Doesn't have skin that's the shade of the purest honey and makes a man willing to sell his soul for just a lick. Doesn't have a sinful body created for the sole purpose of sex and pleasure." He brushed his thumb over her cheek, the bridge of her nose, her mouth. "Doesn't have a wit that can draw blood or make me laugh like no one else can. Doesn't have the ability to have me on the edge of coming just from her voice. Yeah, baby, Candace is beautiful. But like the others, she's not you."

Before she could utter a word—as if she could speak after that declaration—Griffin covered her mouth with his, lips molding and shaping hers to his will. His tongue thrust inside, taking immediate control. He bandied, teased and sucked, demanding she follow him, get wild with him. And she did. Every reason she should protect herself from him, place distance between them, evaporated under the erotic burn of their kiss. God, she'd always loved kissing him. Griffin did it like he fucked: at times hard, at times soft, but focused as if she were all he needed to exist.

She surrendered to the passion he ignited in her with humiliating ease. Spreading her thighs wider, she wrapped her legs around his waist, her feet resting on the muscular curve of his ass. Shamelessly, she rubbed and rode the hard ridge of his cock, moaning at the delicious friction against her clit. Pleasure spiraled out from her sex, and she twisted restlessly under him. Tearing her mouth from his, she pressed the back of her head against the pillow and arched, rolling her hips, grunting at the bump of his cockhead and glide of his thick stalk over the engorged bundle of nerves.

God, it was so good. So fucking good.

Griffin levered himself up, his hands flattening the pillow on either side of her head. He stared down the length of their bodies to the place where his flesh speared through her slickened folds. Lust tautened the skin over his elegant features; it blazed in his eyes and the full, lush curves of his mouth seemed almost cruel in their carnality.

"Fuck, that's pretty," he whispered, his gaze flicking upwards to her face before returning to the apex of their bodies. "That's it. Ride me, like a good girl."

Her sex clenched at his rumbled words, sending a bolt of pure pleasure through her. Making her buck hard, grind against him with no thought but chasing the orgasm that loomed just out of reach. A sizzle took up place at the base of her spine, knotted her belly, pulsed in her clit. Just a couple more strokes…

She cried out as she broke, ecstasy cascading over her. She shook with the force of it, holding on to every throb before it began to ebb, leaving her quivering and still aching. Still craving…more.

"Goddamn, that was beautiful," Griffin snarled, rolling over so her frame draped over his, her still spasming core riding his stomach. He shoved his fingers through her hair, gripping her skull and dragging her down for a furious tangle of tongues and lips. "You've gotten me all wet and dirty with your pussy," he growled against her mouth with a stinging nip to her bottom lip. "Now get down there and clean it up."

One hand remained in her hair, and the other dropped to her shoulder, pushing her down his big body. And she eagerly obeyed. Her just-satisfied sex rippled with renewed desire. She used to love going down on him. Having him fill her mouth with his dense, hard cock. Having him throb on her tongue and swallowing his cum, knowing she was responsible for rendering him as weak as a newborn. A shudder ripped through her as she glided down his torso, pausing briefly for a flick over both flat, small nipples, a not-so-gentle bite to the ridged plane of his abs and laps at indented vee of his hips.

Damn he was beautiful. The sloped, fat cap already leaking clear drops that mingled with the cream coating him from her pussy. The thick, veined stalk with its silky, thin skin. The heavy weight of his balls. He was a hedonistic work of art. Perfect for torment and pleasure. And he gave her both.

Fisting the broad base, she squeezed then stroked her fist up the intimidating length until the crown disappeared inside her fingers. His hips bucked, and he groaned. The first of many sounds she would drag out of him before he filled her mouth and throat with his cum. It'd been so long. And she was starving for him.

Lowering her head, she lapped at the fleshy tip, teasing the small slit before moving down to the column, treating it to long, lush licks.

She tasted herself on him, and hummed, savoring the flavor of them together. With another purr of pleasure, she retraced her route, and for the first time in five years, opened her mouth over his cock and sucked him deep.

"Fuck. Your mouth." He thrust both hands in her hair, cradling her head. "It's so good. Nothing feels this good except that sweet pussy." He traced a finger over her lips—lips stretched wide by his thick flesh. "So goddamn pretty spread wide by my cock. Suck it, baby." His hips thrust forward, burying another inch inside her mouth. "Suck it like you missed this dick for the past five years."

Moaning, she dropped her head over his thighs, and flattening her tongue, swallowed more of him. *Suck it like you mean it. Only your pussy is hotter than this mouth. Fuck it, baby.* Her nipples beaded, and her clit burned at the nasty demands. His cock shuttled back and forth into her, steadily aiming for the entrance to her throat. She hollowed her cheeks, creating a tight suction that had him cursing and uttering dirtier and dirtier instructions.

Again, his hands gripped her skull, and he held her still while he fucked her face with alternating long, slow plunges and short, fast thrusts.

"Open wide for me, Hayden," he rasped. Gliding over her tongue, he slipped his cockhead into her throat. Unaccustomed to the breach after so long, she gagged, the channel tightening, instinctively attempting to expel the intruding flesh. "Shh," he soothed as he'd done earlier. He lowered a hand to her neck and massaged the front with the pad of his thumb. "Relax for me, baby. Relax, breathe through your nose, and let me in."

Inhaling through her nose, she did as he advised, deliberately loosening the muscles in her throat. Allowing him inside her. A harsh groan filled the air, and his blunt fingertips pressed into her scalp.

"Fuck, that was good. Again. Just like that." He withdrew a couple of inches before pressing forward, once more penetrating the narrow passage. And this time he did so effortlessly. She released his cock, digging her fingernails into his thighs as he took over, using her mouth for his pleasure.

And she loved every second of it.

Stroke after stroke, he filled her, claimed her. His flesh swelled and his thrusts quickened, grew fiercer. His choppy breath and almost raw grunts punctuated the air. Excitement and lust surged within her, beading her nipples, tickling her belly and pooling in liquid heat in her pussy. She did this to him—to this gorgeous, male, so powerful animal. Made him lose control. Made him grip her as if she were the only thing anchoring him to this world—to his sanity.

With one last growl, he trapped her head between his palms, holding her steady, and pumped stream after stream into her waiting, open mouth. She hurriedly swallowed every jet of cum, gratefully receiving the evidence of her effect on him. Salty, musky. And so damn delicious. She craved it all.

"Damn it," he whispered, his slightly trembling hands stroking her hair, pushing it out of her face. She lapped at his spent cock, staring up his concave stomach, past his still heaving chest until she met his bright, burning gaze. He grazed her cheek with the backs of his fingers, and when she placed a kiss on his inner thigh, a fine shudder passed over him. "Come here," he ordered, his rough voice brooking no argument.

She crawled up his body, straddled him. Cupping the nape of her neck, he wrenched her down, and his mouth captured hers. Wet, feverish, needy. If he tasted himself on her tongue, it didn't turn him off. Instead, he angled his head and drove deeper, demanding she give him more. And she did. In this moment, drugged by his touch, his taste, his scent, she would give him everything.

Griffin trailed his fingers over her shoulder, followed the path of her spine, and hovered at the base. After a small pause, he continued, feathering a tantalizing, provocative caress down the divide of her ass. Dark lightning lanced her, striking her pussy, and she couldn't smother her whimper.

"No one's had your ass, have they, Hayden?" He pressed a fingertip to her hole, not entering, just teasing her with the threat of it. She stiffened, anticipation and feminine anxiety swirling and clenching her belly. "The man you were with, did you let him touch you here? Fuck you?"

She shook her head. He'd introduced her to the taboo, dirty pleasure. Had made her long for it. Dream about it. She couldn't stomach another man sinking his cock into her ass, stretching her, burning her.

"I want your ass, Hayden. Will you give it to me?" He dipped his hand lower, coated his fingers in her cream then returned to her ass, circling the hole, lubricating it with her own moisture. "Say yes, baby," he murmured.

"Yes." Then gasped as his finger probed and breached the tight circle. Fire raced through her, stealing her breath at the flash of pain. She shut her eyes, breathing past it, as he'd taught her so long ago, pushing back on his finger, relaxing. And soon the pain ebbed, leaving a breath-stealing pressure and aching need that ratcheted her desire past all coherent thought.

His touch disappeared, and she uttered a small, greedy noise of protest. But the sound segued into another moan when he returned, pressing two fingers inside her, stretching her. The pain returned, but mingled with the pleasure, creating a bite that had her pussy streaming, her walls spasming as if screaming for what her ass was getting.

She dropped her head back on her shoulders, arching her back, crying out. Oh God. How could she have gone five years without this ecstasy, this soul-destroying ecstasy?

Griffin grabbed her by the waist, and with a fluent roll, settled her underneath him. And buried his cock deep in her pussy. Unlike the first time, he slid inside her more easily, driving balls deep in one thrust. He withdrew and slammed back inside, a man possessed. Her sex clutched at him, and she clawed at his arms, shoulders, scrambling to find purchase in the erotic storm he'd created. Pleasure careened through her, and she hiked her legs higher, spread them wider, offering all of her pussy up to him. Sucking him had been foreplay, and she was so wet for him, so hot for him, she wheeled toward orgasm fast, spinning out of control.

"Come for me, baby." He rocketed inside her, shoving her closer and closer, his low, strained voice another stimulant to her overly sensitive flesh. "Drown me in this pussy. Give it to me."

Like match to dry kindling, she went up in flames, his demand the accelerant. Her spine bowed, lifting her torso off the bed, her head grinding into the pillow. She shattered with a scream, soaring high, breaking. And he rode her through every explosion, intensifying it, prolonging it.

"That's it," he praised. "You're so fucking beautiful coming all over my cock." He crushed a kiss to her parted lips. "So beautiful."

When the last quiver subsided, he eased out of her body, gently shoving her thighs toward her chest. He leaned over, grabbed a pillow and tucked it under her ass. She glanced down, excitement fluttering in her chest. His cock gleamed with her wetness, and he swept his fingers through her folds, gathering more and sliding it over his flesh.

He palmed her ass, spreading her wide and exposing her hole. Air tickled the entrance, replaced in seconds by the broad head of his dick. She stared up at him, drinking in the lust stamping his features, glittering in his eyes, pulling his mouth into a dark snarl. She needed to imprint this image on her mind for when he was no longer there, in her bed, on top of her, inside her.

"Ready, baby?" he murmured. His gaze flicked up to her, waiting for her nod. "Good. Goddamn, this is going to be so good."

He pressed forward, the tip penetrating her anus. She gasped. Like earlier, pain blasted her, but this time it was sharper, brighter. For an instant, it capsized the arousal, and she almost told him never mind. But, she inhaled, pushed against him, fisted the sheets. Relax, breathe. Relax, breathe. She repeated the mantra in her head until the pain dulled, blurred with returning pleasure and even more pressure than before.

"Okay?" Griffin studied her face, holding himself unnaturally still. She noted the strain his control cost in the lines bracketing his full lips, the almost imperceptible tremble in his frame.

She brushed her fingertips over that grim mouth. "Yes."

His lashes briefly lowered, and he bowed his head, his grip on the backs of her thighs tightening. "Stay with me, baby," he muttered. "I want you there with me."

*Stay with me.* Her heart lurched, the foolish organ taking his plea as something more, deeper than it meant. And damn if she could stop the rush of love that flowed through her. Not when he was steadily pressing into her body, branding her in the most primal way possible. She didn't fight the emotional upheaval, even as she fully accepted his possession. Later... Later when the sweat dried and real life resumed she could go back to denying. But not now.

Griffin worked himself inside her ass, tender but determined. She squirmed and writhed, unable to remain still as each inch gained stretched and burned, the pain intensifying the pleasure. She alternated between wanting to push him away and yearning to pull him closer, demanding more. More. More...

"Fuck." His lips parted, his lashes fluttered as his pelvis pressed to her pussy, his balls to her ass. "So long. All of me. *Fuck.*" His disjointed words scattered around them, his entire length a throbbing pressure in her ass, stealing her sanity.

"Griff," she whined, pleaded. "I need..." She didn't finish the sentence, but she didn't have to. He knew her body, her needs better than anyone else—better than herself.

"Touch yourself," he ordered, his voice hoarse with lust. He plunged two fingers inside her pussy, burrowing inside her with a force that had her keening high and wild. "C'mon, baby. Touch yourself for me. Show me how bad you want me to fuck this tight, sweet ass."

Unable to resist him, she trailed her hand down her chest, over her quivering belly to her sex. At the first touch of her fingers to her clit, she jerked, the rapture of it almost too much to bear.

"Yeah, that's what I want," he growled, falling forward and gripping the top of the headboard so hard tendons stood out in stark relief under his sweat-dampened skin. "I could fucking die in you, Hayden."

He withdrew then snapped his hips, thrusting inside, setting nerve endings on fire that hadn't been ignited since the last time his cock had opened her up. She moaned, circled and rubbed her clit in time with his forceful strokes into her ass. He consumed her, riding her, giving her no quarter, destroying her with each plunge that touched a place she hadn't known existed before him. Her flesh sizzled under her touch, the small nub growing harder, larger. She slipped her other hand through her drenched folds to her pussy entrance and stabbed two fingers inside her, the hungry walls immediately clamping down on the digits. God, it was too much. Too much...

She detonated. Exploded. Imploded. Screams filled her head as she hurtled over the edge into a fire that consumed her, devoured her. And she willingly dove into the flames.

# CHAPTER NINE

If there were different shades of stupid, then she was the fucking rainbow of stupidity.

Hayden groaned, resting her forehead against the shower wall. Hot water streamed over her head, pelting her shoulders, but doing nothing to ease the tension from her body. Which sucked since she'd bought the massage showerhead for that exact purpose. Apparently, the manufacturer meant it loosened muscles and eased stress not caused by spectacular, space-bending sex.

Sighing, she tilted her head back, allowing the spray to drench her face. Behind her eyelids, images of the previous night and early morning flashed by like a Cinemax movie reel. Sinuous heat coiled and snaked through her veins, leaving a path of simmering arousal in its wake. She shivered in the steam, the tremble having nothing to do with the hot water and everything to do with the memories that bombarded her.

*Idiot.* Now that the fog of passion no longer clouded her judgment, she couldn't convince herself that sex with him had been harmless. Letting him into her body had only paved the road for her heart. In the cold light of morning she couldn't deny it. As long as he hadn't touched her, filled her—completed her—she could pretend he didn't have a claim on her heart, her soul. But he'd razed those illusions to the ground with his desire, his overwhelming sexuality and tenderness.

No longer could she blame him for her loneliness or disinterest in other men. It was her. All her. She only came alive for one man; she'd only given her heart to one man. And that man walked away from her five years ago and was preparing to do so again in a matter of days.

She was royally screwed.

Pain throbbed in her chest, and she rubbed a palm above her breast as if it could soothe the ache there. The ache that would only worsen with the coming days, the more time she spent with him. God, she needed space and time to think, to regroup. But since Joshua assigned her to him as his personal assistant, she didn't have the distance to rebuild her defenses.

And she needed to erect that barrier as high as the damn Great Wall of China, because she didn't trust him. Not to stay, not with her heart.

Twisting the knob, she shut the water off and emerged from the shower. Quickly, as if chased by her relentless thoughts, she dried off her body and rubbed the excess water from her hair. Minutes later, clad in her robe as if it were a suit of armor, she entered her empty bedroom and released a soft sigh of relief.

The first time she faced Griffin after their marathon of sex needed to be fully clothed.

The aroma of freshly brewed coffee teased her as she tugged on a faded and ripped pair of jeans and a white tank top. Pressing a hand to her belly in a fruitless effort to calm the nerves tumbling there, she exited her room and followed the scent of coffee like a child trailing after the Pied Piper.

Holy Odin, Thor stood in her kitchen.

After kissing and licking that wide expanse of chest and skin for hours, she should be accustomed to the impact of Griffin without a shirt. But damn. Did one actually become inoculated against the astounding beauty and power of say, the Grand Canyon or the pyramids? And shit, Griffin Sutherland half-naked should definitely be nominated as the eighth Wonder of the World.

And all that dark gold hair brushing his shoulders... Just damn. Since she'd first seen him, the length of his hair had needled her like a puzzle that needed to be solved. Last night, with her fingers gripping the thick strands, she hadn't paid attention, but this morning...whoa.

Who was this man? What made him tick? What motivated him? Who did he love? Hate? Suddenly, the need to know everything about him pulsed inside her like a heartbeat. Because she wasn't familiar with this Griffin. The one she'd grown up with, loved, and grieved had been a brooding, razor sharp, kind and maybe a tad bit spoiled young man. This man though, with his hardened mind and body, older eyes and lumberjack appearance was a stranger. But a stranger she longed to sit with and discover his secrets.

"Hey." Griffin arched an eyebrow. "You okay?"

Shaking her head, she cursed herself and whatever sexual mojo he emanated. "Fine." Doing her best to avoid his gaze, she scanned the counter and noted the carton of eggs, bacon and her waffle iron. Incredulity shoved the wariness aside. "You're cooking?"

He snorted, sliding a cup with steam wafting from the top across the kitchen bar toward her. "Your astonishment wounds me."

She returned his snort. "If memory serves me, the only thing you could whip up was trouble. So please excuse my *What the hell* moment."

He shrugged a burnished shoulder. "It was either that or go hungry. Since I'm partial to eating, I decided on the latter."

"What else can you cook?" She shifted onto the barstool, truly interested in this side of him.

He tugged off a band from around his wrist and gathering his hair together, restrained it in a bun at the back of his head.

Damn. Man bun porn.

He could *so* make it a thing.

"Breakfast is my best meal," he said, picking up eggs and cracking them with easy, expert movements. "Omelets, pancakes, homemade waffles, home fries. But I also do lasagna, macaroni 'n cheese, shrimp primavera, and I can fix a banana pudding that would make you cry."

"I just can't see it." She sipped from her coffee, smiling. "Who taught you how?"

"My best friend and foreman's wife. She took pity on me." He paused, a small smirk tilting one corner of his mouth. "I think she was also afraid I would poison myself if she didn't take me under her culinary wing. She probably wasn't wrong."

Hayden laughed. "Mama always shakes her head and asks herself where she went wrong with me. A daughter of hers who doesn't cook. The horror. The shame."

"I went by the house to see her a couple of days ago."

Frowning, she lowered the mug to the bar top. "I spoke with her yesterday, and she didn't mention it."

He flicked a glance over his shoulder, and after a long pause, murmured, "Were you aware she knew about us?"

Shock ricocheted through her, and she gaped at Griffin. "What?" she rasped. "She...she never said anything..."

"Because you didn't. She'd suspected, but after I left and you..." He paused, his eyebrows forming a dark vee over his eyes.

"Fell apart," she supplied, unable to keep the bitterness from filtering through.

He turned, leaned against the counter and crossed his arms. His intense gaze searched her face, each sweep like a tactile touch to her brow, cheekbones, mouth and jaw. "I'm sorry."

A flippant "Water under the bridge" danced on the end of her tongue, but instead, "For what?" popped out. She briefly closed her eyes, cursing herself. She didn't want to have this conversation. But she'd not only opened the door, she'd thrown it wide and waved him in.

"For hurting you. Hayden, you were the one person in my life who I would have rather cut off my own hand than harm. You were my safe place, my heart. With you I didn't have to pretend to be anything other than who I was, flaws and all. And you accepted me anyway." He glanced away, rubbed a hand over his head and heaved a heavy sigh. When he faced her again, a weariness she'd never seen on him before etched lines on either side of his mouth. "Leaving was...vital for me. At that time it was either go or become someone I detested. I never told you this, but a few months before we became lovers, I walked in on my father having sex with my girlfriend at the time in his office."

"Lauren?" She gasped, shock warring with anger. How could Joshua do that to his own son? And Lauren? Hell, Hayden had never liked the bitch. If she stood in front of her now, Hayden would probably end up as an episode of *Snapped*.

A small, wry smile quirked his lips. "You remember her name. I didn't. Because it wasn't her betrayal that hurt me the most, it was my father's. In that moment, I saw myself becoming him. Selfish, spoiled, self-entitled. And I couldn't allow that to happen. I had to save myself, become a man I would be proud to look at in the mirror. And I couldn't do it here, in Joshua's shadow, under his influence.

"Hayden, you were the one unselfish act in my life. Leaving you was like someone had amputated a limb. It was gone, but I could still feel it; I was incomplete without it. But if I had taken you with me, when I didn't know what waited for me, didn't know if I would be living out of my car or even if where I landed would be my home, that would've been selfish. I wanted the best for you, and at the time, it wasn't me. Stealing your future, your choices... That wouldn't have been love; that would've been greed."

Love. The first time he'd connected that with her. Not even when he'd walked out had he uttered the four-letter word. Grief squeezed her heart. Part of her was glad he hadn't mentioned it then. Because whether he meant it or not, nothing could've stopped her from following him.

"I get it, Griffin," she murmured. "I didn't then, but now? I understand why. And you're right. If I had gone with you, I might not have finished college. I definitely wouldn't be the person I am today. My mother tells me that I'm too strong." She shook her head, huffing out a humorless chuckle. "Maybe she has a point. But I was so desperate to go with you, to be with you, I would've settled for a half-life. I can admit that. I can also admit, you left me...broken. I'd allowed myself to become so dependent on you for my happiness that I was lost without you. The thought of loving someone to the point of, of such desolation and pain again scares the hell out of me. I can't give that power to anyone again, knowing at any time they could walk away, and I would be in that place again. I can't," she whispered.

"Hayden..."

"Why did you cut me off?" she interrupted, the question bursting from her as if catapulted out of her chest. "Before we were...lovers...we were friends. Why did you cut me out of your life like I didn't matter?"

"I tried to call you," he said, and the quiet tone might as well as have been a shout.

She flinched, stiffening and staring at him in disbelief. "No, you didn't."

He nodded, his expression solemn. "I did. Several times during that first year. But you didn't answer, and after a while I stopped. I thought you didn't want anything to do with me, so I gave you what I believed you wanted."

Truth rang in his words, and though they clawed at her, renewing the pain, she accepted them. Believed him. A shudder rippled over her. *Jesus, he hadn't forgotten her... But how... Shit.*

"Mama," she breathed.

Again he nodded. "She admitted it to me."

"Why?" Shock, anger, sadness—they washed over her, drowning her in their deluge. How could her mother do that? She'd witnessed Hayden's devastation... The answer, as clear as a Texas summer day, dawned on her, bright and almost painful in its clarity. "She wanted to save me from further hurt," she stated past numb lips.

"Yes," Griffin confirmed. "When she was at your apartment caring for you, she intercepted one of the calls and blocked my number. She thought she was doing what was best for both of us. Your mother has worked for my family for almost twenty years. She knows them better than most people—*really* knows them. And she understood they wouldn't approve, that they would cause nothing but grief and hurt for her daughter. So when I left, she believed back then that it was for the best."

"She didn't tell me; she never gave me any..."

"She didn't want you to resent or hate her."

Hayden studied his shuttered ice-blue gaze, the stoic expression. "Do you? Resent her?" she rasped.

For a moment, his full lips thinned. "I'm trying not to."

This time, Hayden nodded. The sense of betrayal cut deep, even as she recognized her mother's motivation. Helplessly watching her daughter struggle couldn't have been easy, and her intention had probably been to just stop the pain. But still... Her mother had taken her choice as surely as a thief had snuck into her apartment and stole from her. Who knows what could've been between her and Griffin if their radio silence had been broken through the years?

What ifs. Could've beens. Should've beens. They were pointless. There was no going back. There was only the here and now. And the truth remained in its black and white, stark glory: He was leaving. Again. And sex didn't make them a couple, and it sure as hell didn't make a commitment.

"What are your plans for the day?" She lifted her now cooling coffee to her lips and sipped. Like regrets, this conversation was fruitless except for the pain and anger drenched memories it drug up.

Griffin studied her for an interminable second before turning back to the counter and his abandoned eggs. "Another boring fundraising dinner is on the literal agenda." A pause. "What are yours?"

"It being Saturday, I planned nothing more than vegging out in front of the television with Chinese food and a *Supernatural* marathon on Netflix."

"*Supernatural?*" he scoffed. "Are you serious?"

She tilted her head and scowled. "Breakfast or not, if you're gonna talk smack about Supernatural, your ass has gotta go."

"I'm just saying. There are plenty of other shows on TV. Better shows. More realistic." He snorted. "I bet you, like every other woman, just watch to see one of those guys shirtless."

"Do you practice being that snobby or is it a gift?"

He shrugged, a grin tugging at his mouth and setting her heart off on another gallop down Stupidity Lane. "A bit of both, I guess."

"Have you ever *watched* it?" She jabbed a finger at him. "I bet you're one of those who jeer and scorn but have never even seen an episode. Your ignorance is off-putting. And if it wasn't for the promise of homemade waffles I'd be done with you."

He loosed a low bark of laughter. "I don't need to step in shit to know it stinks and is hell getting off your shoe."

"That's it, skeptic. Let's bet. You. Me. Supernatural. And if you don't like it, I'll ...cook dinner."

A look of exaggerated horror crossed his face. "*How* is threatening me with death a reward?"

"Ass." She snickered. "Okay, if you don't like it, I'll watch whatever asinine, testosterone TV show you deem worthy of viewing. *And* I'll order food instead of cooking."

"Deal." Griffin smiled, and arching an eyebrow, asked, "How do you feel about *The Walking Dead?*"

She groaned.

Shit.

# CHAPTER TEN

"Fuck that. Dean *dies*?" Griffin demanded, glaring at the rolling credits in disbelief. "What the hell?"

Hayden snickered.

He jerked his scowl from the television to the woman sitting beside him. "That's bullshit. After all that, they couldn't find a way to save him? And death by *goddamn* hell hounds?"

She stretched, her white tank top lifting and granting him a glance of caramel skin. Still, even that delicious strip wasn't enough to distract him.

"Careful. One might think you actually became—gasp—invested in the show. That you enjoyed it, of all things." She widened her eyes, all over-the-top innocence.

Okay, so it'd been good. Better than good. Amazing. They'd started watching in the middle of season three where Sam Winchester was searching for a way to save his brother, Dean, from going to hell. A fate Dean had bartered in exchange for Sam's life. And after raising his hopes that the brothers would succeed, Dean died of mauling by fucking hell hounds. He was actually...hurt. So he'd wanted them to make it and have a happy ending. It was Hayden's fault for turning him on to the show in the first place.

Eyes narrowed, he lunged at her, and she shrieked, as he pinned her to the couch. Cuffing her wrists to the couch arm with one hand, he poised the other above her bared belly. "What happens?" When she just offered him a smug grin instead of a reply, he dug his fingers into her skin, tickling her. Her laughter and screams reverberated in the room, and stirred a carefree joy inside him he hadn't experienced in...a long damn time. "What happens, Hayden?" he repeated, dropping his voice to a menacing growl.

"I'm not telling—" Another shriek erupted from her as she wiggled and twisted, attempting to escape him. "Griff, damn it," she gasped, laughing hysterically.

Another "Griff." That made two. Pleasure and triumph escalated in his chest, spreading out like a warm beacon. Last night, when he'd been filling her ass with his cock, she'd called him by his shortened name for the first time since their reunion. She probably didn't even remember the slip. His dick started to harden as he recalled the passion and lust that had suffused her face while he'd fucked her ass. She was one of those rare women who enjoyed the act. How would she react if he confessed he hadn't shared that intimacy with any of the women he'd been with? No one but her. Considering what she'd shared with him earlier, she would probably ice him out.

*The thought of loving someone to the point of, of such desolation and pain again scares the hell out of me. I can't give that to anyone again, knowing at any time they could walk away...*

Her pain had sliced him open. Especially since he'd been the cause of it. She didn't trust him. Didn't entrust anything but her pleasure to him, like last night. And what could he say to ease it? Convince her he would never hurt her again? Never leave her? Both would be lies. Because the reasons he'd left five years ago still remained. There wasn't a life here in Texas for him. And even if by some miracle she opened herself to him again, here was where she'd built her life out of the wreckage he'd left behind. All they had was now.

Forcing the pain down until later when he was alone, he renewed his torture of the gorgeous, wounded, but strong woman beneath him. "Give up the info, woman, or else—"

His cell phone vibrated against the coffee table. Taylor Swift's *Shake it Off* pealed, and he released Hayden and grabbed the phone before it could stop ringing. A certain little girl had programmed that specific ring tone into his cell, and though he grimaced at the looks he received every time it blasted, he couldn't contain his grin. Like now.

"Hey, sweetheart," he greeted Sarah, warmth and love for her flowing through him. She'd called him every day since he'd been gone, and he missed the hell out of her. He tried not to consider the fear scrounging in his heart that something would happen while he wasn't there. Closing his eyes, he forced the thought out of his head, afraid the intuitive girl would catch any sadness in his voice.

Striding from the room toward Hayden's bedroom, he listened to Sarah chatter away about her day, which consisted of treatments and rest but also movies on DVDs, books and video games. Her new obsession was Minecraft, and he laughed as she described the world she was building. By the time they said good-bye ten minutes later, he smiled, but worry edged the joy. Worry for her health, for Jessie and Mary Ann. With Griffin in Texas, Jessie had to man the company on his own, spending more time at work when he should be with his little girl. This devil's bargain with Joshua affected more than just him. Stole from more than just him.

Sighing, he scrubbed a palm over his face, his beard bristling against his skin. Shit. Only one more week, and then he could return home. Slipping the cell in his pocket, he exited the bedroom and padded back to the living room. Late afternoon rays beamed into the room, highlighting the empty couch cushions. He frowned, scanning the area. Movement from the direction of the kitchen snagged his attention, and he pivoted.

Hayden bent over the dishwasher unloading the dishes that he'd cleaned earlier after breakfast. His frown deepened. Her naturally graceful and sensual movements were rigid, jerky. Nothing of the laughing and relaxed woman he'd left on the couch remained.

"Hayden."

She didn't turn around, but continued stacking dishes in the cabinets. "Finished with your call?" The question was innocuous, but the stilted, unemotional tone had him stiffening in alarm.

"Yes." He rounded the bar separating the rooms and grasped her upper arms, halting her before she could bend down for another plate or cup. "What's wrong?"

She didn't meet his eyes, instead stared at some point over his shoulder. "Nothing. I—" Her lips snapped shut, and she squeezed her eyes shut, a spasm of pain flickering across her face. Panic punched him in the chest.

"Baby, what is it?"

With a sound somewhere between a growl and a sob, she wrenched free of his hold. "Stop. Don't." She turned her head to the side, her thick curtain of curls shielding her face from him. "Who was she?"

The whisper, so low and soft, almost escaped him. Almost. Like a movie reel, he rewound the last ten minutes and hit play, seeing what had occurred through her eyes. Damn. He curled his fingers into a fist, his short nails biting into his palm. To her, it would appear as if another woman had called him. And he'd left the room to speak with her, as if she were important, as if she mattered. Which, of course, she did. Just not as Hayden had assumed.

"Hayden, it's not like that." Fuck. He almost cringed. Wasn't that what every busted man used as an excuse when busted? And from her harsh crack of laughter, she'd obviously thought the same thing.

She shrugged and waved a hand, the gesture dismissive. And maybe he would've bought her show of disinterest if she hadn't folded her arms over her chest as if protecting herself. From him. "Doesn't matter. I don't want to know. You don't owe me an explanation anyway." She faced him, that careful mask he hadn't seen since the night in the bar, back in place. He hated it. Hated how she used it to shut him out and disappear behind. "You don't owe me anything."

"Fuck that," he snarled, startling them both with the ferocity that erupted from him. Something primal and possessive snapped inside him, and in one step, he eliminated the distance between them. "Fuck that," he repeated, encircling her arms again in a firm grip. "You don't get to push me away. To lock me out. Not after you've let me back inside your body. Let me have you again. You forfeited the right to push me away the moment you let me fuck that sweet pussy."

"I don't want you," she rasped, her chest rising and falling on fast, harsh pants.

"Liar," he snapped, embracing the pain her words inflicted, allowing it to fuel the lust surging fast between them. He yanked her closer until a breath separated their mouths, and his cock pressed into the softness of her belly. He ground his rock hard flesh against her, his mouth curving into a smile that felt tight and cruel on his lips. "If I slid my hand inside you right now, I bet you would be drenched and sucking at me. Begging to be fucked."

She whimpered, her lashes fluttering down. "I don't want to want you," she clarified on a broken murmur.

Again, agony sliced through him, splaying him open for this

woman. No one could make him bleed like her. "I don't care," he growled then crushed his mouth to hers.

Not gentle or tender. Even if he wanted to, he couldn't give her that. Not with the throbbing ache pulsing inside him like an open wound. He buried both hands in her hair, cocking her head to the side and holding her steady for the heavy thrust of his tongue. She moaned into his mouth, and he swallowed it, demanding another. And another. She dropped her arms from in between them and clutched his wrists. Rising on tip toe, she met him stroke for stroke, lick for lick, suck for suck. It was messy, raw, wet and so hot, his dick pounded with the need to be balls deep inside her.

He grabbed the hem of her shirt and jerked it above her breasts, then yanked down the cups to the pale, flesh-colored bra, exposing her to his desperate stare and touch. He surrounded her nipple, coiling his tongue around the nub and tugging. God, she was delicious. Like chocolate sin. And he couldn't get enough. He switched to her neglected tip and flicked it before drawing it deep, thumbing the other wet nipple, rubbing the moisture he'd left behind into her skin.

Releasing her breast, he slid his hand down the front of her jeans, cupped her and thrust two big fingers inside her. Goddamn, so wet. So tight. Slick, muscular walls clenched him like a vise. She burned and drowned him. He cradled the nape of her neck and tipped her head back, rubbing his mouth over her parted lips. Her thick fringe of lashes lifted, and dark satisfaction poured through him at the hazel depths clouded with passion.

"You're fucking soaked, Hayden," he murmured, curling his fingertips, massaging. She trembled against him, moaned. "You might not need me, but your pussy does."

Her only response was another shudder and a squeeze on his fingers that threatened to cut off his circulation. His groan joined hers, and he tore her jeans open and jerked the denim down her legs. In moments, he had her propped on the counter, his cock in his fist and kissing the plump, glistening flesh between her thighs.

"Take me in, Hayden. Take me inside." Her claim of not wanting him—of not wanting to want him—still scored him like stinging claw marks. This had to be her move, her decision.

He waited, dick throbbing, chest aching from lack of breath. And when her fingers fisted him and guided him inside her, he could've shouted with joy as well as pleasure. She immediately clasped him, embraced him in the sweetest, most intimate embrace. He'd never experienced this sense of welcome, of homecoming with another woman. Sex had never been this fucking important. Like if he didn't sink inside her pussy, he would cease to exist.

Gripping her hair, he gave her head a little shake. "Open your eyes, baby. Look at me. Let me see." Then he sank deep, sheathing himself from tip to base in her. She fluttered around him, dragging a grunt of pure hunger from him. And in her hazel gaze, hot desire flashed. There it was. He withdrew, pushed back in. That's what he yearned to see. That need that let him know he wasn't in this alone.

Over and over, he buried himself inside her, whispering curses and praise about how fucking good she felt sucking his cock deep, about how she took him so easily, about how goddamn gorgeous she was lost in pleasure. Not once did he allow her to close her eyes, shut him out. Wet slaps of flesh smacking flesh, of her pussy releasing and accepting his dick, of their harsh breaths filled the kitchen.

Too soon, orgasm barreled down on him. Electricity crackled down his spine, raced to his balls. Clenching his jaw, he tried to hold it off, wanting to stay in heaven just a little longer. But fuck, it was too good. Too damn good.

Hayden stiffened against him, and enraptured, he watched her face tighten and her eyes darken before going slack with pleasure. Her head tipped back on her shoulders as her pussy clamped down on his cock, milking him. With a low growl, he exploded. Fuck if his soul didn't empty out of him along with his cum.

He rocketed into her, riding her through both of their orgasms until even the ripples faded. Only then did he release her from his gaze and bury his face in her tangled hair. He inhaled her special scent of apples and Hayden.

In that moment, weakened by release, his defenses cracked down the middle, chips falling away. This woman...she'd once been his best friend, his closest confidante and then his lover. His love. He'd trusted her more than anyone. And now, he could continue to protect himself from possible hurt and betrayal or believe in her heart, her spirit, once more.

Closing his eyes, he brushed his lips over the shell of her ear.

"Sarah is an eight year-old little girl," he murmured, taking that leap. "And she's the reason I'm here."

# CHAPTER ELEVEN

Being summoned to Joshua's office like a naughty child first thing Monday morning was not Griffin's idea of a great way to start a day. At thirty years old, he was too old for this shit. And if Sarah's playground and slice of joy didn't hang in the balance, he would've told his father's secretary just that. But his promise was on the line, and it would've been an asshole move to take out his frustration on the woman. Just one more way he and his father differed. One of many he hoped.

The ding of the elevator announced his arrival on the executive floor of Sutherland Industries. A tension that only invaded him when he was in his father's presence seeped into his body, slowly stiffening him as if every cell slowly knitted together to form a barrier within and over him. An unexpected flash of sadness flickered through him. Sadness that he had to guard his heart and spirit when preparing to face his father, the man whose DNA he shared, who raised him, who should've been his role model and best friend. But the same contentious, strained relationship Joshua shared with his father Bud—a need to prove himself, of not feeling good enough, respected—plagued his and Griffin's. A family curse that could've been broken, but hadn't been.

*It will with me.* The steely resolve wavered inside him along with an image of Hayden sleeping among the tangled sheets, her slim arms wrapped around a pillow. He inhaled a deep breath as his gut clenched against the memory. This weekend had been amazing—and agonizing. Pain and pleasure. It'd been more than touching her again, being inside her again. It'd been the quieter moments—watching *Supernatural* with her, laughing with her, cooking for her, talking with her.

But when he'd left her home last night, there'd been a sense of…loss. As if he should've glanced back over his shoulder for one more look. As if he was saying good-bye to something precious. Silly as fuck since he didn't believe in that shit, but he couldn't shake the feeling of uneasiness that dogged him even now.

He thrust his hands in the pockets of his suit pants. He needed to get it together quick. Walking into Joshua's office with any chink in his armor was dangerous. His father could smell weakness like a shark could scent chum.

"Good morning, Mr. Sutherland," the blonde receptionist from a week earlier greeted him. "You can go in. He's expecting you."

Of course he was. He nodded, murmuring his thanks, and entered Joshua's inner sanctum. Like their first meeting, his father sat behind his desk like a king on a throne. Dark eyes studied him as he crossed the room and sat in one of the visitor chairs.

"Griffin."

"Joshua."

Again, another replay. Unlike then, the animosity that had seethed under Griffin's skin like a fire had simmered. Not banked, but cooled so his gaze wasn't clouded by a crimson veil. Maybe because his indentured service was half over. Maybe because his promise to Sarah was that much closer to being finalized.

Maybe because if not for his father's interference, he wouldn't have seen Hayden—been with her—again. In blackmailing him, Joshua had given Griffin the best gift.

"You left Friday's dinner party and missed Saturday and Sunday's events all together. And you didn't answer your phone. I hope you have an explanation for not holding up your end of our agreement."

Griffin arched an eyebrow. "I texted you and let you know I wouldn't make it both days."

"'Something came up' is not a satisfactory reason."

"It was the best one I had," Griffin said. "I also apologized for not making them."

"Not good enough, Griffin." Joshua templed his fingers underneath his chin. "They were important and your presence was required."

Struggling to rein in his temper, Griffin didn't immediately reply, but paused several seconds. "I've attended every party, dinner, opening, and exhibit on your list. Sometimes twice a day. I've held up my end of the bargain exceedingly well, Joshua. I'm certain I didn't sabotage your family image because I missed a gallery opening and a tea."

"That wasn't our agreement. In exchange for the deed to the property, you agreed to comply with my expectations and instructions, which included appearing at every event set in the itinerary. You failed to do so."

The combination of Joshua's calm tone and ominous statement knotted Griffin's gut. He knew his father, was familiar with his tactics. And Griffin's instinct screamed Joshua was circling, readying himself for the kill.

"Did you call me in here just so you could scold me, Joshua?" Griffin cocked his head to the side. "I can tell you're going somewhere with this, so why don't you just get to it?"

At the flicker of satisfaction in his father's eyes, that unease exploded into full-blown dread.

"By not fulfilling your obligations, you broke the contractual agreement," Joshua said evenly...smugly. "Therefore it is null and void."

*Null and void. Null and void.* The three words seemed to echo in the office over and over until they deafened Griffin, pounding against the inside of his skull. His heart slowed, thudded dully in his chest as rage boiled in his gut like a cauldron seconds from spilling over. Heat flushed his skin, and he curled his fingers around the arms of the chair in an effort not to lunge out of it. If he left the seat, he wouldn't be responsible for his actions.

"You're. Fucking. Kidding. Me," he stated, voice quiet but no less hard. No less bitter.

Joshua's eyes narrowed, but the warning for Griffin to watch his tongue didn't come. He leaned forward, his black gaze gleaming with triumph. *Good for you, you son-of-a-bitch. You got one over on your own son. Fucking daddy of the year.*

"A contract is a contract. You didn't follow the terms, so I'm not obligated to either. That was your choice, not mine. I don't know how you do business, but I'm not nearly as lax," he sneered.

"What do you want, Joshua?" Griffin snapped. "Because I know you, and you want something other than to rub my nose in your superior business sense. What pound of flesh must I give this time?"

"You stay in Houston."

"I intended to do that anyway."

"Indefinitely."

A silence thick with shock and anger rippled between them. *The fuck?*

"What the hell are you talking about?" Griffin demanded. "You want me to remain here until a time you deem is satisfactory?" He barked out a harsh crack of laughter. "Is the governor's seat that important you would hold your son hostage?"

"Yes," Joshua bit out. "It's important. It's legacy, heritage, loyalty and duty. Something you have still managed to learn nothing of. Goddamn it, Griffin. You are a Sutherland. As much as you have tried to forget that in the armpit of Florida where you've holed up for the past five years. I've given you enough time and a long leash. It's time for you to stop playing business man and come back to your family and be one. A real one. Take your place where you belong."

"Is that what this is all about?" Griffin whispered, the truth dawning on him with the power of an anvil to the chest. Ice spread through him, its frigid fingers creeping across his chest and up into his throat, freezing his lungs and breath. "Forcing me home?" At his father's silence, Griffin shook his head, another hoarse chuckle escaping the deep freeze his body had tumbled into. "Do you hate me that much?"

Joshua slashed a hand through the air, a scowl darkening his face. "Don't be ridiculous. This is about family."

"What family? We weren't a family long before I left. Your idea of love is control until the point we bend, break or run away. You demand loyalty, but you've never offered it to us unless we conform to your idea of right or wrong, acceptable or contemptible. You can't even give your wife fidelity, but you command we sacrifice it to you unconditionally. Your idea of teaching me how to focus on my career and make it my priority was *fucking my girlfriend.*"

"Are you kidding me, Griffin? That was years—" his father growled.

"Ago. Yeah, it was. And I don't give a damn about her. The lesson I learned that day was I had to leave or become the kind of man who would give his son life lessons by fucking him over. *You* pushed me away, Joshua. *You* ran me away. But even then, instead of being proud that I created a successful, thriving company out of nothing, you can only think about ripping it away from me. About destroying it because you don't deem it worthy."

Joshua slowly rose to his feet, color flooding his face, fury thinning his lips. "I know what it's like to want to prove yourself, to be your own man. Why do you think I left Sutherland Industries all those years ago and went to work for your mother's father? I understand the need to leave a mark. But, dammit, I've worked hard all these years so you and your brother and sister would have that soft place to fall, not have all my years of work thrown in my face. Regardless of what you think about my method, Griffin, I love you—all of you, and I've only wanted you to succeed."

"According to your definition of success. Under your control." Standing, too, Griffin faced off against his father, and even though his father's words scored a hole in his heart, the desk might as well as have been a divide keeping them on opposite sides, separated. "For all your *work*, Dad, your soft place was the hardest and most unforgiving of them all."

Something deeper, heavier than anger settled inside him as he stared at his father. Grief. For who they could've been to one another. For the relationship they would probably never have. For…them. Inhaling, he turned and headed for the office door.

"If you leave, I will not sign over that land to you. And we both know how much it means to you."

Griffin paused. Pivoted. "What do you mean by that?" But even as he asked, he already knew the answer. That sense of foreboding from earlier returned, hollowing out his gut.

"The playground. Sarah Montgomery."

Pain blazed through him, incinerating organs. How had Joshua…? Griffin had only told one person about Sarah…

*Hayden.*

But even as her name popped into his head, seconds later he dismissed it. She wouldn't betray him by revealing something so personal and private to his father. *Of course she would*, logic argued. *She's loyal to him first and foremost. She works for him.*

But his heart clung tenaciously to the trust—to the love—in his heart for her. No. Five years of hurt, disillusionment and regrets lay between them like skeletons on an ancient battlefield, but she wouldn't betray him. Not like this. She wasn't the woman who had screwed his father behind Griffin's back. She wasn't petty, mean, grasping or a liar. An image of her from a couple of days ago again flickered across his mind's eyes. Fierce and pissed on his behalf when he'd revealed what his father had done all those years ago. Honorable. Kind. Wounded, but trustworthy.

Besides, there had been one other person who had been aware of his plans for the property. The seller. Griffin hadn't concealed his reasons for desperately wanting the land from the owner, hoping the purpose would sway him. He probably wouldn't have seen any reason to not tell Joshua.

"It's not going to work, Joshua," he murmured. "Would I pay you ten times the money the land is worth to keep my promise to a sick little girl I love? Absolutely. I was willing to cater to you and your will for two weeks even though this is the last place I would rather be. But I'm not going to sell my soul for it. And because Sarah and her parents love me without strings attached or for what I can do for them, they will understand. That's what family does. That's what love does."

Turning once more, he left without looking back.

***

Damn it, she was running late.

Jabbing the key to Griffin's townhome-slash-office, Hayden unlocked the door and stepped inside. Not that her coma-like sleep should've been a surprise considering she'd had precious little of it this weekend. A smile tugged at her lips as she dropped her purse and bag on the living room couch. Heat curled low in her belly, and she pressed a palm there as if it could quell the delicious swirl. Nor could she smother the annoying but insistent urge she'd woken up with. The need to lay eyes on Griffin. To inhale his midnight and earth scent. To be surrounded by his big, hard body.

God, if she was this hungry for him after one week of daily interaction and two nights and days of hot, mind-blowing sex, what would she be like come this Sunday when he returned to Florida?

Cold doused her like a bucket of frigid water, immobilizing her.

Memories of endless, lonely, empty days flooded her mind. Of half-living like a zombie. Of the clawing grief that almost destroyed her.

Jesus, she was headed toward the very thing she feared and vowed wouldn't happen.

"Hayden."

She blinked, dispelling the pictures from five years ago that bombarded her, and focused on Griffin. Where had he come from? Shaking her head, she briefly closed her eyes. *Get it together.* She had to get. It. Together.

"Hey." She cleared her throat, quickly scanned his white dress shirt and black pants, and glanced away. "I received your text about a meeting with your father. I didn't expect you to be back so soon." A few minutes. That's all she needed to compose herself, form a make-shift shield around herself until she could retreat to her apartment and fortify the badly crumbling wall surrounding her heart.

"I'm leaving."

Déjà vu. It hit her so hard, she swayed and clutched the back of the sofa for support.

"*Shit.*" Griffin lunged for her, but she slammed up a hand, palm out.

No. He couldn't touch her. Not now. Not ever again.

God*damn.* Sucking in a deep breath, she straightened, forcing herself to stand on her own power, to face what was coming.

"Hayden," he growled, stepping toward her in spite of her warning. Her palm pressed into the solid wall of his chest, and unable to help herself, she curled her fingers into the dense muscle.

*Stupid.* She snatched her arm down, crossed both over her chest.

"What happened with Joshua?"

His hooded, brilliant gaze studied her, but thank God he didn't try to touch her. She might lose the frayed and tattered remnants of control she maintained.

"Because I missed the scheduled events this weekend, he reneged on our agreement. If I want the property I'll have to stay here in Texas and join Sutherland Industries."

Shock reverberated through her like a discordant note, loud, painful and just wrong. How could Joshua treat his son like a...a chess piece to move over a board at his whim and direction. Many times since she'd started working for him she'd witnessed his often ruthless business tactics. But Griffin wasn't a rival for an oil lease or a hostile takeover. He was his son.

"I'm sorry," she whispered, clenching her fingers into fists. Either that or reach out to him and stroke the harsh lines etching his face.

"Yeah, so am I." He shoved his hands into his pants pockets. "He even knows about Sarah."

Okay, just when she believed the market on surprise had been cornered. "How…" Then she flinched, shaking her head. "Griffin, I didn't…" She couldn't finish the sentence.

But she didn't need to.

He frowned. "Baby, I know."

Relief poured through her, and she exhaled a breath she hadn't been aware of holding. "Thank you," she rasped. "I wouldn't hurt you like that."

"Since he refuses to budge, there's no point in my staying. There's nothing here for me."

Pain unlike any she'd experienced since that night five years ago blasted through her. Her lungs and heart constricted, and a swarm of dots invaded her vision, buzzed in her ears.

*There's nothing here for me.*

The flat statement joined the drone in her head, and bile raced for the back of her throat.

*You knew this. Why are you surprised?* She shook her head as if answering the waspish voice in her head.

Because a tiny, foolish part of her that still believed in castles and princes on white steeds had hoped he would stay this time. That she was enough to keep him here. *Idiot. When will you learn? When will you let go?*

"Hayden." Firm fingers grasped her upper arms. Gave her a small shake until she opened her eyes. Griffin stared down at her, the blue of his eyes so intense it was almost tactile. "Come with me." He released an arm and cupped her face in a big, warm, calloused palm. "Come with me, baby."

The need to turn her cheek into his hand, to kiss it shivered through her…and made her tear free of his hold.

She stumbled, quickly pivoting and crossing the room on unsteady feet. Once she reached the big window in the living room, she pressed her palms to the glass, heedless of the prints her damp skin would surely leave behind.

How could three words sharpen the agony until it sliced through her like the razor edge of a blade? *Come with me.* What she wouldn't have given to hear him utter the request five years ago. Her future.

Her plans. Her soul. She would've given it all. But that was then when she didn't understand the devastation of depending on someone, of making them you're everything only to have them take it away. She couldn't do it again. Couldn't risk it.

Couldn't take a risk on *him* again.

"Hayden."

She hadn't heard him come up behind her. His heat called out to her, invited her to turn and lean on him, allow him to shelter her, care for her.

She straightened her shoulders. And her spine. "I can't." Silence met her decision, and she pushed on. "You want me to give up my life, my career, my plans. To do the very same thing your father asked of you. And you refused."

"No," he said, voice quiet, solemn. "Joshua demanded. I'm asking. Asking you to choose me."

"And then what?" She loosed a flat, jagged laugh. "Go to Florida and depend on you for everything? Pin my dreams, my path, my identity on you? Been there, done that, have the T-shirt and broken heart to prove it." Her fingers curled into fists against the window. "No. I can't let you wreck me again." Shut up. Have some pride. But the seal on the dam had been cracked, and the hurt, the desolation, the anger poured forth. "I won't let you destroy me again. I won't hand you that kind of power over me again. Never." She choked on a sob, tears burning her eyes. "I won't love you again," she rasped.

His hand covered hers, clenching tight. For several moments, she stared at them. Together. She understood what he was saying without saying it. He would cover her, protect her, shelter her.

A lie. But one she desperately longed, fucking *yearned* to grab a hold of and believe like Moses had brought it down a mountain on two stone tablets. With a low, keening cry that seemed to well up from the depths of her soul, she ripped free of his "promise" and whirled on him, slamming her palms into his chest.

The fingers of one hand wrapped around her wrists, imprisoning her hands against him, while the other cupped the nape of her neck.

"Stop it, baby," he snapped, the hard, angry tone contradicting his tender touch. "You're fucking killing me." Pain laced the low rumble, but she didn't care. Was beyond caring.

"You didn't come back for me. You didn't want me. Didn't love me enough to come back." The tears leaked past her lashes and trailed down her cheeks in a searing, damp path. "You never came back for me," she cried, breaking. Crumbling. Her knees buckled as she sobbed, losing the battle against the years of pent up grief and hurt and loneliness.

Swearing, Griffin swept her up in his arms, cradling her in his lap and against his broad chest. How long she cried, she didn't know. But the entire time, his strong arms remained around her, rocking her, as he murmured nonsensical things in her ear, pressed soothing kisses to her hair and forehead. And when the fury eased, he continued to hold her, only leaving her once to wipe her face with a warm washcloth.

"I'm sorry." The emotional storm had taken a toll on her voice, the rasp hoarse in the silent room and tender against her throat.

"Never apologize to me for that, Hayden."

She lifted her head, met his gaze. Though no moisture clouded the blue depths, he sounded as harsh and rough as she did.

He swept the pad of his thumb over her swollen eyelids, down her still damp cheek and trembling mouth.

"I love you." The quiet statement echoed in the room, the power of it rippling like a boulder thrown into a still, placid lake. "I've always loved you. First as a boy, a friend, and then as a man so terrified of fucking up the one precious thing in his life, he chose to leave rather than ruin her. Before I ever took your body, you stole my heart. It's only ever been you. It will only ever be you. From the moment you came up to me at seven and smiled like I was the most important person in your world—like I was your world—I was yours. You loved me not because you had to, not because of my name but because you wanted to. You loved me unconditionally, fuck ups and all. You were—are—the one pure, good thing in my life. Proof that I'm not the selfish, spoiled screw up 'spare' that I've always seen myself as."

He tunneled his fingers through her hair, cupped the back of her skull as if she really were the precious thing he called her.

"What I told you was true. I did try to call you, and when I couldn't, I convinced myself my decision had been right. Because in those moments of weakness, if I had reached you, I would've said to hell with sacrifice and not fucking up your future. I would've begged you to come to me, to forgive me. To love me. Like I'm doing now. Hayden." He sighed, and she fisted her fingers against the urge to soothe away the weariness in the heavy sound. "You're wrong. I came back for you. When you walked up to me in that bar, you sealed your fate. I stayed away all those years because I loved you, but when you found me, all bets were off. Joshua gave me a convenient excuse, but property or no property, I would've come for you."

A vise tightened around her heart, and the traitorous organ stuttered against her rib cage. But fear—oily, pervasive fear—coiled around her tongue, stilling it. Invading her and choking her.

"You don't have a reason to trust me, to believe in me. And I know in my desire to give you everything you deserved I hurt you. Broke your heart. But, baby, take that step toward me and let me put it back together. Yes, I'm asking you to leave your home, your job, your plans. But I'm not asking you to depend on me for your happiness. I'm asking you to depend on us for it."

He lowered his head, brushed a kiss over her lips and pressed his mouth to hers for a long breath. Then he gently lifted her from his lap and walked out of the room. Headed to the bedroom where he would pack his bags and leave.

Again.

But unlike last time, he wasn't abandoning them.

She was.

# CHAPTER TWELVE

"Dad told me you were resigning. I didn't believe it, so I had to come see for myself."

Hayden glanced up from the desk drawer she was emptying of the personal items she'd collected over the years she'd worked for Joshua. Josh stood in front of her desk, staring down at her, a dark eyebrow arched. She hadn't seen him since their exchange at the charity gala two weeks ago. The gala she'd attended with...

Swallowing hard, she skidded away from that thought. It'd been a week since he'd left for Florida, and she could barely think his name much less speak it.

Shrugging, she placed a spare make-up kit and handheld mirror in the cardboard box on top of her desk. It was after five, and the Sutherland Industries executive office had emptied of employees. Even Joshua had left an hour ago for a meeting. So much for packing up and escaping without a confrontation.

"Yes, it's true."

A corner of his mouth kicked up, but those fathomless dark eyes, so much like his father's, remained on her, shuttered.

"I would say this was a surprise, but then I would be lying."

She paused, the framed picture of her and her mother in hand. "I'm sorry?" She hadn't decided until last night that she was quitting, so how had he guessed?

"I figured when Griff returned it would only be a matter of time before you left."

The shaft of pain stole through her, quick and bright. She froze, regulating her breath so every lungful didn't feel like a handful of razors slicing her open. After a moment, she carefully resumed her packing, placing the picture in the box, her fingers lingering over the glass.

The morning after he'd left, she'd been stunned to realize she could move, could function. The grief and loss formed a lodestone in her chest, so huge she had to work to breathe around it, but... But she hadn't been shattered.

While the bright morning sun beamed into her bedroom windows, she accepted that she was no longer that vulnerable, young twenty-one-year-old. At some point in the five years she'd strengthened, had learned how to survive even when a hole had been carved out of the place where her heart used to be. She was stronger, and she could—she *would*—make it. She had no choice.

Being happy was another matter altogether. Strength apparently didn't equal happily ever after.

"I hate to disappoint you and your father, but I don't base decisions concerning my life around Griffin."

Nope, she reserved those choices for fear.

Damn, could she slap her own self silly?

"I never said you did. And if Dad claimed that, then he's wrong." Josh crossed his arms. "Can I ask why you are resigning?"

She sighed and leaned back in her office chair. She and the heir apparent had never been close, so why he'd searched her out to find out her plans boggled her mind. Ever since Griffin's return, he'd been real chatty with his cryptic statements wrapped up in questions. Too bad for him that since she'd quit, she no longer owed him a polite "kick rocks."

"Me first." She tilted her head, narrowed her eyes. "Why do you suddenly care? Since I started working for your father I can count on one hand the number of times we've talked. You damn sure have never been interested in my personal life. So why now? So much that you waited until after five to search me out."

He didn't even blink at her surly tone, just slipped his hands in his pants pocket. And in spite of the difference in their coloring, reminded her so much of Griffin, she had to glance away. God, when would things, people, scents, goddamn *breathing* not remind her of him?

"Because I wanted to tell you it's about time. And I hope you're happy."

"Okay, wait. What?" she blurted, taken aback.

"Griff and I haven't exactly been...close over the years. That's an understatement. He saw my path as putting my nose up Dad's ass, and I saw his behavior as that of a petulant spoiled brat. No, we definitely didn't see eye-to-eye." A wry smile curves his mouth. "But one thing I always did admire about him was your love and support."

"Josh—" she breathed.

But he waved off her objection. "I saw it; I've always seen it. As he grew older and no matter what he did, you remained by his side, I started to look at him differently. I have you to thank for that, Hayden. If not for your devotion to him, I would've never bothered searching beneath the tough, rebellious exterior to see the hurt, rejected and brilliant kid that captured the heart of one of the kindest persons I knew. If you loved him, there was more to my brother than what he elected to show people. And I was happy he had you. Even after he left home, I believed you two would somehow end up together again. I didn't think it would take five years, but at least it's finally happened. Because you need him just like he needs you. You haven't been as happy or as free in the past few years as I remembered. I'm glad you'll have that again."

Shock robbed her of speech. Hell, air.

"When do you leave?"

"I'm not," she whispered.

He frowned, and she finally detected emotion in those eyes. Anger. Disappointment.

"What? Then what's this about?" He nodded toward the cardboard box.

She pinched the bridge of her nose and sighed. "Over the last week I've realized I'm not a good fit here. I can't...agree with some of the decisions your father makes. And by continuing to work for him, I'm silently abiding them. I'm not that person. And even a well-paid position in Sutherland Industries, possibly for the next governor of Texas, isn't enough to convince me to be that person."

"And you hadn't figured this out two weeks ago?"

*Before Griff returned home* lay unspoken between them.

Gritting her teeth, she said, "No."

"I never took you for a coward, Hayden."

The bald, flat statement again halted her, rocking her back against her chair.

"Excuse me?" she snapped.

He didn't flinch at her biting tone or the healthy amount of "mind your damn business" in it.

"I've watched you face down my father at his angriest. Witnessed you handle difficult clients without ruffling a feather. Only the strongest sort of woman could manage to earn a position as my father's personal assistant without fucking her way in and remaining off her back. I respect you. And it's because I do that I'm calling you on your shit." He planted his palms on top of her desk and leaned forward, his black gaze pinning her to the office chair. "You. Are. A. Coward."

"You don't even know me," she snarled, shooting to her feet. Damn if he would make her cower. "I don't care whose son you are, you—"

"Love my brother," he interrupted with a snarl of his own. "We don't have to be confidantes for me to notice how you look at him. The same way you always have. With love. And for some reason you'd rather stay here alone than go after what, *who*, you want. That makes you a coward."

"I-I," she stuttered, the fight, the denial, the anger draining from her, leaving her weak. *Christ*. What was she *doing*? She flicked a glance at Josh, for the first time really *seeing* him.

The loneliness. The pain.

"You would so cavalierly throw away what most people will never have the gift of experiencing. Of having," he murmured, his stern face solemn.

God, he was right. Out of fear, she was ready to live a half-life of grey rather than a full, sometimes terrifying one of vivid, shocking, overwhelming and gorgeous color.

A life with Griff.

One that was hers if she had the balls to grab it.

Yes, she would be starting over, but it wouldn't be as a naïve, young girl who didn't know who she was or what she needed. It would be as a woman who'd gone through hell to get what she wanted. And that was him.

It was *them*.

"Thank you," she whispered.

A smile ghosted over his lips, and with a nod, Josh left.

She grinned. Laughed. And with an energy—a hope—she hadn't possessed in years, she continued packing.

She had a man to get.

# CHAPTER THIRTEEN

"Ouch. Son-of-a-bitch," Hayden grumbled, rubbing the throbbing in the toe she'd just stubbed against a box.

"Language, Hayden." Lorena Reynolds tsked.

"Sorry, Mama." Hayden winced, grinning. "Hey, have I told you how much I appreciate you coming over to help me pack on such short notice?" Her mother's hmmph came across the cell line loud and clear, and Hayden grinned. "Seriously, though, Mama. Thank you."

Lorena cleared her throat. "You're welcome, sweetie," she murmured.

The night Hayden had returned home from the office, she'd called her mother, and they'd finally spoken about her confession to Griffin. Lorena had apologized, explaining she'd been trying to protect Hayden, but had been wrong for interfering. Though hurt, Hayden had understood, and had told her mother so, as well as her plans to follow him to Florida. Lorena hadn't been surprised, and, years later, fully supported her. Had even come over the following morning to help Hayden pack. Her mother's concern hadn't eased, but she also realized Hayden had to live her own life. A life that included Griffin.

"Well, I'm just about done. I have a few more odds and ends, but for the most part I'm ready to pull out in the morning." She propped a fist on her hip and scanned the living room. Most of the knick-knacks were in boxes, waiting for the moving company to store them and the furniture in storage. In the foyer, several boxes and bags waited for her to place in her car for the long drive to Florida.

A tangle of nerves twisted and tumbled in her belly. Yep, she was driving all the way to the state she'd vowed never to return to just two weeks earlier. And she would be a liar if she claimed she wasn't nervous as hell. She'd just packed her apartment—her life—up in four days and decided to move across the country. So yes, there had been a few moments in the last few nights when she'd stared at the ceiling and asked herself, *what the fuck?* But then she pictured Griffin's face as he asked her to trust him, to trust them.

Yes. She wasn't leaving Texas as much as running to her future.

"Remember what I said about stopping in lighted areas and making sure you make it to the hotels well before dark," Lorena lectured.

Hayden snorted. "I'm even going to pray for Jesus to take the wheel somewhere around Alabama."

"That's not funny, Hayden," her mother snapped.

"Yes, ma'am." She swallowed back a bark of laughter. "I promise—" A knock reverberated on her front door. "Oh, let me call you back. Someone's at the door. Love you."

Still chuckling, she ended the call, set the phone on the back of the couch and headed for the door. Rising on her tip toes, she glanced through the peep hole. "Who is...*Oh my God!*"

She yanked the door open and flung herself into Griffin's arms.

Hard, strong arms encircled her, pressing her into a solid wall of a chest. She wrapped her legs around his waist, planting kisses on his bearded jaw, chin and finally, his mouth. His warm laughter brushed her lips, his big hands cupping her ass.

"What are you doing here?" She demanded, leaning back in his arms, grinning up at him. This...this humongous, ever-increasing air in her chest that seemed as if it could elevate her to the ceiling...this was happiness. Joy. It'd been so long, she'd almost forgotten.

"You're here," he rumbled the simple explanation, shifting forward into the apartment and kicking the door shut behind him.

In three steps he had her back pressed to the wall—the same wall he'd made love to her against a couple of weeks ago. With his hips wedged between her thighs, his chest pressed to hers, his cock notched against the heart of her, she was safe, sheltered, protected. Right where she yearned to be.

His mouth covered hers, their tongues mingling as his tongue parted her lips and sank deep. God, his taste. She'd missed it. Angling her head, she opened wider for him, tangled her fingers in his hair, underneath the bun of cool, thick hair.

"Fuck, I've missed you," he growled against her lips, echoing her thoughts before returning for another hard kiss.

"Me, too," she murmured, smoothing her fingertips over his forehead, his high cheekbones, the sinful mouth. "I can't believe you're here."

"Where else..." He trailed off, surveying the foyer and the living room. His eyes narrowed as they skipped over the boxes and bags. "What the hell is all this?" He returned his gaze to her, the blue brilliant, piercing. "Hayden?"

"I'm packing."

"Packing?" he whispered.

She nodded. "Yeah. Tomorrow I'm leaving." She smiled. "For Florida."

His grin was slow, but blinding. "Florida?" He tipped his head back on his head, laughing. "And here I thought I was going to have to camp out on your couch until I could convince you to change your mind."

"You came back for me," she murmured, wonder, love and joy rising inside her like a tidal wave.

"I told you. All bets were off." He nipped her bottom lip, soothed the small sting with his tongue. "But you were coming to me."

"Yes. I love you." She cradled his face between her palms and stared into his eyes. "I'm so sorry I didn't tell you before you left. I'm sorry you had to go one day believing I didn't love you, because I do. I've never stopped. It's always been you for me, too, Griff." He closed his eyes, a breath shuddering from between his lips. "Always."

"That's three times you've called me Griff," he said, his voice low, rough. "Say it again."

"Griff," she whispered. "Mine."

"Always," he whispered back. "Always."

# READ ON FOR AN EXCERPT FROM NAIMA SIMONE'S

# ONLY FOR A NIGHT

# LICK, BOOK 1

*About Only For a Night*

Rion Ward fought hard to be free of the Irish mob life. Now, as the co-owner of Boston's hottest aphrodisiac club, he's traded crime for the ultimate sexual fantasy. But when the "good girl" from his past walks through Lick's doors, he discovers that his unconsummated hunger for her never abated.

Widowed for two years from a man who felt that anything besides the missionary position was dirty, Harper Shaw is ready to move on. The first step to feeling alive again is sex. Hot, dirty, black-out-from-orgasm sex. And who better to provide it than the brooding, sexy, tatted bad boy-turned-man she's known for years?

Rion, however, has one stipulation: He'll be hers only for one night. One night to explore her every fantasy. One night to push her limits. One night to introduce her to a passion that makes both doubt if it will be enough...

*Excerpt*

"What are you doing here?" The deep, midnight voice sliced through the memories, and Harper willingly locked the vault on them. Rion's velvet tone slid over her exposed skin like a velvet caress, resonating in her chest, curling in her belly—and lower. "I asked you a question," he said, the demand silky but no less menacing.

"I-I came here to speak with y-you," she stammered. God, she sounded like an idiot. "I hoped we could talk."

A black eyebrow arched high. "Talk," he enunciated, a corner of his sensual mouth curling into a faintly sardonic sneer. "What could you and I possibly have to talk about?"

"I—" She peered over his shoulder, for the first time noticing the blond giant standing behind Rion. Sasha. Sasha Merchant. A close friend of Rion's. "Would you mind if we... Can we speak in private?"

"No."

She reeled back on her death-defying heels, teetering before grabbing the table tighter. "No?" she repeated. Seconds of silence passed between them. Irritation warred with mortification, and she tilted her chin in spite of the heat rushing up her throat and into her face. "That's it? Just no?"

"Yes."

She sighed, exasperated. "Rion..."

"Go home," he interrupted, the order unyielding, hard. Dismissive.

"Rion, please," she murmured, cringing at the plea that crept into her voice.

"Sasha, would you mind escorting her safely to her car?" He turned, again disregarding her without hearing her out.

Anger shoved the hurt aside, surging hot and hard inside her. She'd been dismissed, shelved, or patronized too often in her life. She'd also been mute, opting to remain silent, not rock the boat. Not voice her needs, her wants...her desires. Well, that time had passed.

She was tired of living—no, existing—in a cocoon that was supposed to be safe but was really suffocating.

And he didn't get to push her back into that cocoon.

Aiming a dark scowl at Rion, Sasha stepped forward, his hand extended toward her. "Sorry, sweetheart—"

"Wait a minute," she snarled, skirting past Sasha and latching onto Rion's arm, ignoring the sexy flex of muscle beneath her fingers and palm. Rion froze, probably in surprise rather than from her hold. "We were friends for a long time. Too long for you to just toss me aside like a stranger. Okay it's been five years since we've seen one another. You can at least give me five seconds."

Slowly, Rion pivoted, dislodging her hand. Staring up into his lean face with its stark lines and stormy eyes, she shivered. Fear had picked a fine time to remind her the absolute stupidity of stirring a predator.

"Five seconds." He slid his hands in his pants pockets.

"Thank you." She sighed, relieved. "If we could just—"

"Three," he stated, his tone past bored and veering into catatonic.

"I need you," she blurted. Damn. Oh God. Just…damn.

His eyes narrowed. "What do you need me for?"

"I can't—" Panic crawling up her throat, she shot a glance at Sasha who didn't even pretend not to be absorbed with the scene playing out before him. "Rion," she whispered.

"Two seconds."

"Damn it. Sex. I need you for sex."

For the first time, Rion lost his stoicism, shock widening his eyes and parting his lips. Beside him, Sasha sounded as if he were being strangled, and her? She squeezed her eyes shut, flames bursting inside her, consuming her in a conflagration of humiliation. Jesus Christ. Was death by mortification possible?

"Oh fuck," she groaned.

"Yeah," Rion drawled. "I got that."

Yes. Definitely possible.

# ALSO BY NAIMA SIMONE

# ABOUT THE AUTHOR

USA Today Bestselling author Naima Simone's love of romance was first stirred by Johanna Lindsey, Sandra Brown and Linda Howard many years ago. Well not that many. She is only eighteen...ish. Though her first attempt at a romance novel starring Ralph Tresvant from New Edition never saw the light of day, her love of romance, reading and writing has endured. Published since 2009, she spends her days—and nights— writing sizzling romances with a touch of humor and snark.

She is wife to Superman, or his non-Kryptonian, less bullet proof equivalent, and mother to the most awesome kids ever. They all live in perfect, sometimes domestically-challenged bliss in the southern United States.

Connect with Naima through email (nsimonebooks@aol.com), through her website (www.naimasimone.com), on Twitter (https://twitter.com/Naima_Simone), on Facebook (https://www.facebook.com/naimasimoneauthor/), through her newsletter (http://naimasimone.com/contacts.html) or become a member of her fabulous Facebook Street Team (https://www.facebook.com/groups/376601019163211/).

Made in the USA
Lexington, KY
13 January 2018